DRIFT

DRIFT

William Mayne

JONATHAN CAPE
THIRTY-TWO BEDFORD SQUARE LONDON

First published 1985
Reprinted 1986
Copyright © by William Mayne 1985

Jonathan Cape Ltd, 32 Bedford Square, London WC1B 3EL

British Library Cataloguing in Publication Data
Mayne, William
Drift.
I. Title
823'.914[F]   PR6063.A9/
ISBN 0-224-02244-X

Printed in Great Britain by
St Edmundsbury Press, Bury St Edmunds, Suffolk

For Elly

one

The Indian girl was trying to catch a crow that had stayed in the village by the lake all winter. The girl's name was Tawena, and she lived in the tents and cabins at the end of the village.

Rafe Considine watched her, sitting on a heap of hard snow outside his own door. Tawena was throwing down little balls of suet from a lump of fat she had in her hand. Now and then she ate some herself. She had a fatty face, Rafe thought, and brown eyes deep in the fat. He was sure she had stolen the suet. The tent and cabin people had nothing much to live on, but some of them were well-covered.

Tawena made throaty noises towards the crow. The crow came nearer and picked up a little nut of suet. Rafe was eating a crust. He threw down a crumb of it for the bird. It walked towards him and ate it.

Rafe thought he would go into the house now. But when he began to move the girl told him to keep still.

"Don't move, Rayaf," she said. "Don't do ever thing. Bird for pot." She dropped down another fragment of waxy fat, and the bird came nearer.

Rafe waited. He wanted to see what happened to the bird. Inside the house his mother put wood on the stove and smoke dropped down the roof to the ground.

"Wind has changed," he said. The bird looked at him. Far off a rifle was fired, where someone else was hunting.

The bird did not notice that. But from the direction of the lake, a little later, there came a louder noise, like a bigger gun. The crow did not like that, and just when Tawena was about to stretch out two hands and grab for it, it jumped and flew up to the roof, where it walked about having a good look.

The Indian girl was not disappointed. "Ever day," she said. "Some ever day, crow and pot," and she nibbled the suet. She came and sat beside Rafe. He could smell the suet now, and it was bad, rancid. He decided she had not stolen it – it must have been thrown away from one of the houses or stores.

"We go get look at bear," said Tawena, and she offered Rafe a piece of suet. "Bear my people father."

At that moment, before he had to decide what to do about the suet, which he could never eat, or what she meant about the bear and her father, the door of the house opened and his mother came out.

"You lift off my step, Indian girl," Mrs Considine said, putting her toe against Tawena. "Don't you be playing with the likes of them heathens from the cabins, Rafe, I've told you."

The Indian girl went away, and the crow flew off.

"And what was the noise?" said Rafe's mother. "Oh, the smell of that child, and I'm not fussy! Rafe, what was the noise? Is it the French coming back up the river?"

By now Mrs Considine was not the only person out of

the houses asking what the report had been.

"It's a cannon," said one, and "It's the Frenchies for sure," said another; and a third was saying "Maybe it's us giving them what for," and wondering what with. But the village manager came from his office and asked whether they didn't remember that the ice broke in spring, and all they had heard was that, some great crack on the surface of the lake as the water level dropped or lifted.

"Spring, is it?" said Mrs Considine. "Rain instead of snow – is that a blessing?" She went in, giving Rafe a look meaning he must have nothing to do with the Indian girl.

Rafe thought he wanted to know what Tawena meant by looking at bear. He had seen bears in the woods, and heard one in the village at night, trying to get at stores, and there were bearskins in the warehouse. But to go and look at one is something different, even with someone you don't at all like, smelling of old fat, even if she is the bear's daughter, somehow.

Tawena was round the corner of the house. The bear was not with her, of course, and Rafe was glad of that.

"Where is it?" Rafe asked.

"On lake shore," said Tawena. "Come get look, Rayaf. I show."

Rafe thought the snow was cold, and the wind was cold. When he was near the house he could go in when he wanted and get warm. Tawena lived in a tent, with the fire outdoors. She kept warmer because of her leggings with the fur inside. Round her shoulders was a blanket for a shawl. Rafe was not sure he wanted to go in this weather to the lake shore at all.

"On," she said, taking his hand in her greasy one. He took it away. He did not mind the tallow, which was a thing he often had on his hand from a candle, but would not hold a girl's hand.

The village was on the shore, but in winter there was no

way of telling that, because the water was ice, solid from the land, with the same snow on it. Tracks went on to the ice, and a long way out was a little hut, where men went to fish. Men were out there now, and smoke coming from the hut.

The bear was not here, but along the cliff. Tawena went in front. Rafe thought she had been this way before, because there were footprints, and not of a big person either. She followed them exactly, a foot in one and a foot in the next, a straight line.

"You walk like me," she ordered Rafe, when she saw how he kicked his own way along. So he walked along in the same single track.

They went up and up, until the lake was below them, and the village away behind. Rafe thought he could jump down to the lake if he had to, and run back to the village. He made up his mind not to go away from the shore, or out of sight of the houses.

The shore curved round. After a time the village was not behind them any more, but over to the left. He could see it across the frozen lake. They were walking towards a headland, going so far round that at last the hut on the lake was between them and the village.

The wind blew more and more from the south, up the lake, a cold wind. At first it had been behind them, and as they turned it flew in their faces, and stung. Snow was being carried along with the wind. There was noise too, other loud shots like cannon fire, and a great grinding out on the ice.

"We'll go home," said Rafe.

"Get look at bear," said Tawena, plodding on, one foot in front of the other. Snow melted on her high cheeks.

Then there were no footprints ahead and none behind either. All had filled with snow. The girl walked on.

The snow grew thicker, and the wind harder. Rafe

shouted that they would not see anything in this weather. Tawena walked on more slowly. She stopped at last. Rafe could see nothing now, and walked into her. They both fell down where they were, and the wind shook them.

There was more noise than the wind could make alone. Something else was moving out on the lake. The ice was shifting as the water lifted and dropped it. A splinter of ice came whirling out of the invisibility and cracked against Rafe's left shoulder. When he looked round he saw, close against him, the ice rising, climbing the cliff, moving in the storm.

Now the ground itself began to shake under them. All at once Rafe could not tell where he was, where he had come from, how much time had gone by, whether it was day or night, or whether he was alive or dead.

He could see the girl's brown eyes. She sat there calmly, nibbling the same piece of rotting suet, and she was waiting. "All go," she said, but she had to shout it against his ear before he understood.

Then the snow stopped coming from the sky. It still blew along the ground, lifting from it, but below them the lake was swept clear of it. There was a great mound of ice blocks, heaped like houses against the headland. The ice still moved and shook the ground. Towards the middle of the lake, beyond the flat ice, open water moved in waves.

On top of the cliff, at the end of the headland, something moved that was not ice. Something climbed out of a place behind a rock, and stood up, looking, something dark. It was a house-length away.

"Bear," said the girl. "Bear out. We go, we go, we go soon, we go."

"Where?" said Rafe. There were no footprints to follow.

"Go on ice," said the girl. "On lake. Bear on land. Bear not asleep. Bear out. Go, run, Rayaf."

They could not go on to the lake from this point,

because the broken ice-heap was moving below the cliff here, grinding and snapping and growling. Rafe thought of the bear, waking sourly from its winter sleep, thinking it might eat them, grinding and snapping and growling at them too.

They hurried back along the cliff. Rafe led the way, not caring where his feet went, not making a neat single track. The girl clung to the back of his coat.

On the headland the bear saw, or smelt, and followed. They stumbled and tumbled against the wind, through the snow and cold, until they were beyond the broken ice, beyond the place where the ground shook. As soon as he could Rafe went over the edge, not caring that the girl still held him and would have to come too before she was ready.

Then, landing in a snowdrift, they found they were out of the worst of the wind, the bear was high above them, and between them and the village was only a stretch of clean ice. Even if they were tired there was the hut of the fishermen halfway to home.

They joined hands and they ran. There was still enough wind to bite them, and they could feel the ice tremble as they went, but they knew it was thick. Behind them they heard the great blocks tumble and break against the cliff.

They looked round, and the bear was gone from the sky-line. Rafe's feet caught on a step in the ice, and he fell, but the girl lifted him up, and hurried him along. Rafe looked for the step, but it was no longer there. It had been made by ice lifting and lowering, up and down.

Something seemed to be wrong. They were still running down the lake towards the hut and the village, but the village was no longer there. It had skipped far over to the left. Rafe did not know why that could be so, but it did not matter, because the fisherman's hut was straight ahead of them. He could smell the smoke of its stove.

12

They came up to it, and stood in the shelter of its wall, and it was warm to be out of the wind, though they were still outside. That was only until the wind came round the hut and blew on them again. Then Rafe knew that the hut had turned round. It had turned round because the ice it stood on had come loose, and was no longer fixed to the shore. They both felt the ice sway under their feet when they stood still.

They went into the hut, because that was the next thing to do. They went in and closed the door. They could hear each other now.

The stove was burning, there was bacon hanging on a hook, a fish on the table, wood to burn, but there was no one here, no one to make them feel better, to make them feel rescued. Rafe looked out, clearing some snow away that held the door open. And there, looking back at him, was the bear, sniffing towards the hut, not afraid, hungry, wanting the bacon and the fish, and ready to take it. They were alone on floating ice with a hungry, fierce, selfish animal, a bear woken from winter sleep.

two

The bear looked back at Rafe. Rafe stood and looked at the bear. He did not know what to do. He knew there was something he could do, something simple, but he could not remember what it was. He could only remember that a brown bear was standing on all four feet just outside the door. He could smell it, and it could smell him.

He remembered that he could shut the door. But the trouble was that his arms had forgotten how to work. He wanted to tell Tawena to shut the door for him, but his voice had gone. He had forgotten how to speak.

He stood in the doorway and saw the bear walking towards him, because his eyes were still working even if his arms would not.

A small yellow-white thing, as big as his fist, rolled out beside him through the doorway, and stopped in front of the bear. The bear stopped walking and looked at the thing, and turned it with its nose.

It was Tawena's lump of suet. Now Tawena herself hit

the door hard and slammed it, and the latch caught.

"Bear," she said, as if Rafe had not noticed.

By now Rafe found his eyes had stopped working. The hut was dark and the window black. Then he thought his legs had gone through the ice, because they felt cold. But they had only stopped working too, which made him sit down suddenly. He knew that he had fainted and felt ashamed of doing it in front of the Indian girl.

By the time he felt better Tawena had put wood on the stove and laid the fish on the griddle top to cook.

Rafe began to find he could move when he wanted. He felt he was not strong. He was cold underneath where he sat on ice. Gradually he kneeled up. Arms and legs and eyes and voice would work now. His mouth worked too, because as soon as his nose smelt the fish cooking his tongue grew wet and hungry and he wanted to eat.

"Is it ready?" he asked. Tawena turned and looked at him angrily. She made a hissing noise with her tongue, and he knew it meant "Hush" and that he must keep quiet. "Bear," she said. "Bear listen."

Rafe thought the bear was outside now, and there was nothing to worry about.

He felt the floor sway a little. He first thought he might be faint again, and then he remembered that they were in a hut on a piece of floating ice. The ice was not joined to the land any more, and no one would walk out from the village and send the bear away.

"All the same," he thought, "we are safe inside. We are in, the bear is out, the door is shut."

Tawena held a piece of hot fish out for him. He pulled off warm flakes of its meat and put them in his mouth. He was hungry, and the fish was very good to eat. He came to the stove and he and the girl ate all the fish. When Rafe had finished the girl sucked the head of the fish, the tail and the fins, then ate all the insides, and quite a lot of bones. She

15

left only the thick ones down the back, dropping them in the stove. She licked her hands for a long time.

Rafe licked his. Inside the hut the fire crackled. Outside the wind blew and ice banged. When Rafe wanted to speak to Tawena she hissed at him, through the fingers she was licking.

Rafe knew he must not make a noise. He climbed slowly up on the table. He was now beside the piece of hanging bacon. It swayed from side to side. Rafe found that he was swaying too, keeping his balance as he stood on the table to look out of the window.

There was wind and snow outside, and he could not see far at all. Everything was white, or white with shadows under it.

The shadows were blue and grey, and now and then they were so dark he could not tell the colour at all.

One shadow seemed to stay where it was but grow bigger. It was difficult to tell. The glass in the window was of a rough sort to start with, and there was snow outside and steam inside. Rafe's head got very warm up in the top of the hut.

The shadow he was watching grew bigger still. It seemed to spread in the glass.

It was a brown shadow. It was not a shadow at all. It was the bear coming closer and closer, sometimes roving on all fours, sometimes rising on its hind legs, seeking, sniffing.

"Bear," he said.

Tawena hissed at him, just reminding him to keep as quiet as he could. She went on licking her fingers. She silently took a billet of wood and put it on the stove.

"If it wasn't for the bear," Rafe thought, "we should be warm and comfortable, and we've had a good meal."

The bear went out of sight, round the hut. It went out of Rafe's mind too, and he jumped off the table with a thump. As he jumped he despairingly remembered that he should not have done it. The girl was too cross with him to hiss. She looked and looked.

Rafe began to look too. He naturally looked at the door, which was where he had seen the bear, and where he himself would have come in. But Tawena listened all round.

They both heard. They heard the bear snuffling and sniffing along the bottom of the hut wall, down behind the stove. Perhaps the smell was strongest there.

The bear huffed and breathed and blew. It began to scrape at the snow and ice outside. Claws hit the wooden wall of the hut, like nails being driven in.

Then it stopped snuffing at one place and went all along the wall, from corner to corner. It began to bite the corners of the hut, high up the wall, and right down at the bottom.

Inside, Tawena and Rafe listened and watched. The wood was planks, not logs, nailed at the corners to an upright post. The bear was pulling at the lowest planks, easing the nails out, and digging under the angle.

The floor began to give way, because there was a hole outside. Cold wind came in. The bear's claw showed. Tawena went to stand quite close to the place. Rafe went to the far corner. He could feel his heart clattering inside him.

The bear stopped digging at the corner. It came breathing round outside the hut, pawing at the walls. It had a particularly long look at the door, where there was a crack between the door and the frame. It breathed up so much air that Rafe thought it must take it all from the hut. It knocked on the door three times, like a person. Rafe thought he should open it, because it must be a person come to rescue them, but Tawena glared at him and he stood still.

The bear did not knock on the door again. Rafe began to think it had gone away. He moved towards the table and

17

the girl hissed gently. Rafe thought the bear would have come anyway, even if he had not jumped off the table; but he would not jump down next time.

He got up once more, and looked from the window. He thought it must be near nightfall, because the hut was getting darker quite quickly.

Then he saw that the darkness at the window was the bear's shoulder and back. As he stood and watched the bear turned the back and the shoulder, and there was his head, and his eye looking in, looking back at Rafe's eye, with his head turning from side to side.

The bear could not see into the darkness of the hut. But it could still smell that something was in there. It dropped down from the window.

Rafe climbed down from the table. The girl watched him.

"I think it's going away," said Rafe, standing by the table, speaking in a whisper.

"Bear stay," said Tawena. "I know bear. Bear my people, my . . ." and there she waved her hands from side to side, because she did not know the English word. Rafe thought she meant something like God, but he did not think there would be claws and a smell like bear. Tawena must feel like that about the bear, because she was not frightened, only quiet. But, he remembered, she had been frightened once, out on the headland.

Now there was quiet for a time. Rafe sat on the table. The girl licked her fingers.

Outside the bear began to run, or perhaps it was digging deep and quick. Whatever it was doing it suddenly hit the back of the hut, behind the stove, hitting so hard that wood cracked, the stove tipped, the chimney split, and there was fire over the floor and smoke everywhere.

The fire was all they had to stop them dying in the night. At once they lifted the stove back, burning their hands, not caring. In the north countries fire is the first friend in the frost. They picked up the fire itself and heaped it back into the hearth. Rafe jammed the chimney back as near as he could get it, but the hut was full of smoke, and smoke came in more and more.

The bear came to the door again. Here it found it could sniff underneath much better than along the walls, and it found it could dig better too. It sniffed and dug. Inside the hut Rafe sneezed with the smoke. The hut swayed on the moving ice. There was a smart crack as the floe broke somewhere not far away.

Rafe thought, quite clearly, that when the fire went out they would die of cold, but before that the ice would break under them and the lake would drown them. So there was no need to worry about the bear.

He was wrong. At that moment the bear decided to rear up and knock the whole door down, so suddenly that Rafe had to jump aside.

When he looked the door was on the floor, smoke was flying out through the doorway and cold air coming in. The bear was standing half in and half out, having a look round, deciding what to do next, quite certain it would be able to do it.

three

The bear licked its lips. It showed yellow teeth. It dribbled stringy dribble.

Rafe watched it. His mouth was too dry to move, his tongue was like leather. The bear was very close, the length of the door away from him. If it took a few bear's paces it would be touching him.

The bear thought about things, still deciding what to do next. It had its front feet on the fallen door, and now it moved its paws like a cat. It did not like the way the door shook under its weight, and was not sure whether it was safe to walk on. It brought its back legs further forward. Rafe thought it might jump right along the length of the door, and be in the middle of the hut.

The bear had been thinking about the door lying loose on the floor and perhaps being a trap. It had also been looking round. What it saw, and smelt, and wanted, and had come in for, was the bacon hanging from the roof. That was where it looked.

It gathered its back feet together again. Rafe was sure it would jump now.

Tawena had been standing the other side of the stove, watching. Rafe turned his head and looked at her. He wanted to say something, but the words would not unswallow themselves. Tawena was standing there doing nothing. Rafe had the feeling that she was not properly afraid, and he thought she should be, because he was. Then he saw that her yellowish face was paler than it had been. He saw that she was breathing fast. He saw that her mouth was very tight shut, but her chin shook a little bit. He saw that she was frightened. Rafe did not want her to be frightened, because that was disagreeable for her, and made him more frightened than he had been.

Even the bear was still worried by the way the door rattled on the ice. It was still making up its mind, but the girl had made hers up. She left her place by the stove and walked to the doorway.

She walked on the door lying there. The bear said something in its throat, and lifted a front paw. The door twisted, and the girl went on walking along it, taking short steps.

She walked right up to the bear. Rafe felt that was all wrong, that she should not do such a thing, that the bear would hit her. He wanted to say that they should give the bear the bacon.

He did not have time. Something more frightening happened, and then something so strange that he could not have expected it, and neither could the bear or the girl.

The bear rose up on its hind legs, filling the doorway. It was actually standing just outside, where its back legs already were. It had not gone away from Tawena. Rafe could tell it was getting its paws ready to crush Tawena. First Tawena, then him, then the bacon, Rafe thought.

A strange thing was happening to the bear. It stood quite

21

still, watching Tawena. But it began to grow smaller, and to go away. It was not walking. It filled less and less doorway, and was not so near.

"Gone away bear," said Tawena, as if nothing odd was going on. "Put door." And she stepped off the door and began to lift it up.

"But what is it?" said Rafe. "What is happening?"

"Ice break," said Tawena, not thinking anything odd had occurred. "Bear float away."

Rafe felt that he was floating away too, as if his senses were not much good any more. But the piece of ice the bear had stood on, close to the door of the hut, had broken away and carried the bear off. The bear was now the far side of some ripply water, and back on all fours again, sniffing the ice, wondering what had happened to the bacon it had seen. Rafe understood how it felt.

A slop of water came in at the door and froze on the floor. Rafe looked out. He thought the ice must have broken where the hut's posts had been driven into it when the hut was made.

Now, outside, the air was filling with snow and hail. The bear was going out of sight. Rafe felt the cold wind coming in.

He and Tawena lifted up the door and put it in its place. It was not an easy thing to do. The door was wide and heavy. The floor they stood on was slippery. It would not have been difficult to let the clumsy thing slide out into the water. But they got it up, and Tawena held it while Rafe brought the table up to it. That was not the simplest matter, either, because the table's legs had frozen down to the floor.

"Bring pork," said Tawena, when the table was loose. Rafe climbed up again and lifted the bacon down and let it lie on the table. Then they jammed the table against the door, and it stayed.

22

The wind was locked out of the hut again, and even the broken chimney did not fill it with smoke now.

Rafe had his knife in his belt. He wanted to cut some bacon now, while he could still see, because darkness was coming on. He would be hungry soon, he knew.

Tawena would not let him. "Eat ever day," she said. She meant that tomorrow would be soon enough for the next meal, and that they must go without for tonight. Rafe put the knife away, and licked his fingers instead. They tasted of salt and fat, but raw.

Darkness came. Outside the wind howled. Inside the hut there was a glow from the fire. Rafe wanted to make it a big flow, a fine blaze. But again the girl would not let him. She let the fire go down low, heaping ash against the charcoal. "Not ever wood," she said. "More ever day."

The hut became cold. Of course it was spring time now, and there was no deep frost. Rafe thought there might be no frost at all that night, but it was not a warm night. They stayed awake almost all through it. There was nothing to lie on but the ice floor of the hut, and though that was covered with a layer of ashes, and chips of wood, and was hairy with straw, it was still smooth with cold.

All night long the hut rocked on the water. Once or twice Rafe felt quite sick with hunger and the swaying. He leaned on the cooling stove, and the girl leaned beside him. Sometimes he walked across to the table and touched the bacon. Sometimes he could not abide the thought of it. Tawena stayed by the fire, now and then laying wood on it.

Daylight came slowly. When it did, the wind did not seem to be so noisy. And the air grew warmer, because Tawena raked ash away and put a log to burn, making the stove hotter again.

Rafe looked from the window. He had to climb the wall to see anything, and then he could not see it clearly. He thought he saw lake, and might have seen hills beyond the lake, with trees on.

He thought they might be near the shore where they started from, close beside the village.

The girl allowed him to slice bacon off the piece. She put the rough slices on the griddle, and they began to get warm. Fat dropped into the heat of the fire and flamed. There was the smell of cooking bacon.

Rafe thought of the bear. Could the bear smell it? Then he thought he heard the bear growl, but it was his stomach, standing up and feeling like a bear.

They had a slice of bacon each, hot on their hands, the grease running down into their palms to lick up later.

When they had finished the slices, and were licking the fat up, the hut began to buck about again, in rough water. Rafe thought it was fun at first, and wedged himself against the wall, because the shaking was enough to make it easy to fall over. In a little while, as the shaking went on, he wished he was not licking bacon fat from his hand. A little while after that he wished he had not eaten anything at all, because he felt dizzy in the head and hollow under the chin. And just as he knew he was bound to be sick, worse happened, which made him forget about it.

There was more than one thing.

The first was the loud noise of ice breaking. The ice that broke was the floor of the hut. It snapped from corner to corner, between Rafe and the stove. The edges of the crack lifted and fell, making a step along the floor. Water came up from below and ran about.

The second was that the table slipped away from the door, and the door fell over, twisted, and went out of its own doorway.

The third was that the brightly glowing stove tipped over and fell on the floor again, as it had done when the bear hit the wall.

24

Rafe thought they could deal with that, because they had dealt with it before. But this time the floor broke and melted under the stove, and made a great steam and hissing, and with a bang and a crack and a thud the stove went through and down into the lake, leaving only some floating sticks and charcoal, taking all the fire with it.

The chimney fell into the hut and rolled on the floor.

It stopped rolling. All at once the hut had stopped moving and the floor became solid once more, except for the crack and the hole. Rafe got up and walked about. Tawena looked out of the doorway.

The hut had struck land. There was a stretch of water beyond the doorway, but not far off was land with snow and bushes.

"Ah," said Tawena, with an Indian grunt. She picked up the bacon and pushed the table out of the doorway. Rafe went to help, and between them they made a bridge across the water to the land, walking across the table.

There they stood, in the snow, with a cold wind and a clear sky.

A little way off, the bear climbed out of the lake and came towards them. Tawena threw the bacon towards it. The bear took it in its mouth and walked away. It had what it wanted.

"No food, all lost," said the girl. "We die ever so soon."

She sat on the trunk of a fallen tree. "No mans here," she said. "Land of bears, all ever bears."

four

Rafe looked round him. He and Tawena were standing on the cold snowy shore of a half-frozen lake. To one side were rocks and bushes, and a little further off trees and then hills, all covered in fresh snow. It was spring snow, so thick on the branches that it fell off lump by lump, making a noise like people walking, making Rafe think hopefully that help was coming.

The girl thought differently about the walking noise of the snow. She looked about with a great and slow caution, working out what each sound must be before turning her eyes anywhere else.

On the other side the lake was floating with ice, blocks and floes of it, with moving water between, splashing up when a drifting floe struck another. They rattled like stones. Among the pieces of ice now floated the door, water washing it. Then the table itself got off its legs when it was nudged and turned on its back, sailing away with its legs in the air. Between the current and the wind it spun and twirled and seemed to be waving goodbye.

The hut, on its patch of ice, joined in the movement. Its floor opened up, and the corners of the hut came apart, stretch by stretch, like trousers splitting open. Rafe watched. The nails drew out creaking. He grinned at the sight.

Tawena was keeping a look-out against danger. She was not watching things that could be amusing. She listened; she searched the ground, kicking the snow aside, picking up stones, wanting a particular one.

She found it at last. She spoke to Rafe, saying an Indian word he did not know. When he did not understand her she moved her hands about, and he understood that she wanted his knife. He did not want to give the knife to a girl, but she was the one that knew how to do anything. He wanted to see what she did. By now he had seen enough of the slow splitting of the hut, and was becoming much colder than people could get, he thought.

The girl took the knife when he pulled it from its sheath. Rafe thought for a moment that she was going to cut into the stone she had picked up and find some wonderful thing to eat, some strange rich sweet egg, perhaps.

She was going to find something from the stone. First of all she took out from her sleeve some fluffy moss, dry and grey. She padded her hand with it, filling the palm, and held the stone against it with her fingers. Then she started to tap the stone with the knife.

Rafe was angry at first, because hitting stone with a knife is the way to spoil the knife. But he knew what she was doing when he saw a spark fly from the stone, or the knife. He smelt the spark. It happened again, and this time he smelt the moss burning. And a third time there was a little glow in the tinder. The girl breathed on it, but it went out. She tapped again.

Rafe looked round under the snow for small twigs, pulling with white cold hands at thorns and spikes. All the matted stuff round the roots under the snow was dry. He scraped and dug, and hurt his fingers, scratching the backs of his hands.

Tawena did not think he had done well. He could tell by the way she looked at him that she thought he was an ignorant rough savage. Before she began striking sparks she had neatly gathered a bundle of twigs, and had it ready.

She looked at what Rafe had done. "Bear," she said. "Ever mad bear." Then she was too busy breathing into her hand to say more. She looked about, she blew. Rafe looked at the ugly marks he had made on the ground, and he looked where Tawena had taken her twigs. He could not see that place. He looked where his feet had been treading about. It was like the fight of the mad bear, he thought. She was right. Tawena herself had made three little footprints as she came from the lake, and she still stood in two of them.

I go about breaking the world to pieces, thought Rafe.

Then there was smoke in the air, and the little snapping of twigs where a sudden hard flame stood on the girl's hand. She knelt down and put the fire on a flat stone. She carefully looked at the mat of rubbish Rafe had dug out, taking a few pieces from that, and there was fire he could feel, smoke he could see.

He felt that things were about to come right, now they had started to keep warm.

On the lake the hut had creaked open all the way up to the roof. The roof split along the ridge and fell in.

Tawena still looked about anxiously. Rafe thought they could keep the bear off with fire now.

"Get ever bit," said Tawena, pointing to the hut with an Indian sign, looking and pushing out her lips. Rafe understood that well enough. He thought the hut would make a

28

good fire and keep off any bear. All the same, he did not like going into the icy water to fetch it. As well as that, the pieces of the hut were still huge, made of whole sides of wall and of roof. The door and the table, which he might have brought, were now afloat and far away.

The girl hissed at him, although he had not spoken or made any noise. All he had done was think, and he did not see how she knew what he thought; and he was right anyway.

"Rayaf," the girl whispered, as if something dreadful had happened, as if, perhaps, the bear had come back and he had to do something about it.

He turned to look at her. She was listening, looking, feeling out for something she had to know.

Rafe looked and listened with her. There was nothing new that he could tell; nothing had changed in the bushes under the snow, nothing moved among the trees on the far hills. Only the distant falling of snow and flutter of branches went on, and that had been there before, and he was used to it.

"Indian womans come," said Tawena. "They kill Indian girl right off. They kill you with Indian girl, Tawena. Tawena go away, you ever see Tawena again, ever see Tawena, ever. This white boy fire. Tawena ever at village."

Then, all at once, she had gone, ducking under the branches of the bushes, out of sight in a few seconds, leaving Rafe alone with the fire.

She had taken his knife with her.

He knew then, for certain, that it was just a trick, and that all she wanted was the knife. He was sure she was going to join her own people, because this was her side of the lake, her part of the land. He knew she had left him to die, and that there were no Indian women.

He followed her track for about four footprints. After

that he could not tell where she had gone. Without her there was no sound of people at all, only the rattle of ice on the lake, the dropping of snow from the trees, the cold wind, and the little running of flame in the tiny fire.

He crouched by the fire. He forgot about the bear. He forgot about Tawena. He remembered only how very hungry he was, hunger worse than cold, cold worse than fright, fright worse than anger.

He took a handful of the fire stuff he had gathered and put it on the fire. The fire made a great sudden smoke and very nearly went out. Rafe had to kneel down in the snow and breathe on it very carefully for a long time before it recovered.

And when he stood up, with runny eyes, and coughing like a moose, someone was looking at him. He first thought it was Tawena, because it was an Indian's face. But it was an Indian woman, much thinner. Rafe's heart missed a beat, he thought, when he saw her, and he was so glad to see someone it began to race. Then everything slowed down, because the Indian woman was not looking at him in any friendly way at all. The way Tawena had looked when he made a fine mess of fire stuff was scornful and even unkind. But it was better than the way he was looked at now.

The Indian woman hated him. He did not hate her. But he could tell he was her worst enemy, and that at any moment she would kill him. And that was what Tawena had said: Indian women would kill him.

He turned to run away. He would run into the lake, along the shore, away from this woman. When he tore his eyes away from hers and turned to run he was at once held by another Indian woman, who had come silently up behind him, and who now held him by the hair with one hand and with the other took a firm grip on his ear. When

30

he struggled even the slightest amount she pulled his hair with one hand and the ear with the other, as if she would pull one out and the other off. Rafe had to keep still. He was crying with pain.

The Indian women stamped his fire out, and looked round the place where he had landed. He had made so much mess in the snow and under the bushes that they did not think of looking further away for Tawena.

They tied Rafe's hands behind his back, with leather thongs round his thumbs, and led him away, one ahead and one behind, taking him through the rocks and bushes towards the trees and hills.

He had to walk steadily in the footprints of the woman in front. When he trod clumsily the woman behind him hit him with a stone; when he fell over she hit him with two stones.

She had a stone in each hand. As they walked along she clicked them together, slower than walking, and each time there was a click she gave a whispery hiss. The woman in front did not look round at all.

They walked for a long time and came under the trees. Far away among them was their camp, an untidy skin tent. Rafe was made to sit in front of that, and the camp fire was made to blaze. The woman who followed him sat in front and finished tapping stones together. She had been chipping one stone into a knife with a ragged sharp edge. She was pleased with it.

There was a smile on her strange Indian face, a grim smile. She put the knife in her pouch. Then both women left him lying in the snow, and went away. The fire drooped in its hearth and stopped throwing out any warmth.

Round about, in the forest, snow fell from the trees. Small animals moved on the ground and in the branches, and between the trees moved larger animals he did not know the names of. They came close to the smell of Indian and white boy, then puffed the scent from their nostrils and went away. Rafe would usually have liked to know about them all, watching and learning their comings and goings.

But now he did not care.

five

Rafe was now so miserable he did not know what to think. He had forgotten there had been better times, and could not think of having once had them. He thought that things would always be bad for him now, that they were now worse than they could possibly be.

He was cold right through himself, in spite of the fire not far away. His legs ached from standing up all night. His head hurt from being awake all night. His insides felt horribly trembly and had a pain, perhaps from being hungry or from eating the wrong thing. Worst of all, his thumbs had died where the leather lace was tied round them, so he could not tell what held his hands together behind him; and to make up for it his arms had cramp in them, and were pulling up and down on their own.

He stood up, thinking he could walk away, even run away. But he fell over and could not get up. He was lying on his side in the snow. Every time he cried, which he couldn't help doing, it hurt him all over and he could not breathe. Every time he stopped he started again.

After a time he found that he was crying without sobbing. Tears ran straight out of his eyes and dropped on the ground, melting the snow. His nose ran too, and he could not wipe it.

The tears in his eyes made the fire appear to sink and swell, come closer, go further away, be brighter, be darker; and darker and darker.

Rafe fell asleep.

When he woke he was looking up into the trees. He was not comfortable, but he was no longer in pain. Everything was there just the same, but he had become used to it.

High in the leaves of the great pines there was a glitter of sunshine, which made him think everything would soon be much better.

At the fire the Indian women were cooking. Rafe watched them. If he was an Indian, he thought, this would be like home, with fireplace and food. He looked at the two women. Their faces were wide, with high bones under the eyes; like Tawena, but she was fatter in the flesh.

He felt angry at Tawena for a moment, remembering how she had taken his knife by a trick. Then he remembered it had not been quite a trick. She had run away to stop herself being killed, she said. Rafe recalled that the Indians living in their own places did not like the Indians who came to live in the village. But it had been Tawena's trick. Why had she not taken him with her?

He thought about being killed. So far it had not happened. He looked at the woman with the stone knife in her pouch. She had a cloak made of the skins of hares. The other had a coat made from deerskin.

Hareskin looked at him and said something to Deerskin. Deerskin looked at him too. He remembered that Indians do not smile much, but he thought that Deerskin nearly smiled, and Hareskin did not smile at all.

34

He did not have any smile to use back on them.

When they had cooked they ate their food. They were eating long black things. Deerskin put some of the long black things on a sheet of bark and put the bark beside Rafe's head.

"Eat," she said. Rafe did not know the word in their language, but he understood it. And the long black things smelt good.

He had to wriggle across to get at the bark plate. The wriggling was very painful again, and he heard himself groan and squeal as he moved. But he got to the right place and put his head down to eat with his face in the food, because his hands were still behind his back.

The long black things had legs. They had eyes as well. But they were cooked, and hot, and smelt good. And most things you eat have legs and eyes, though not usually so many legs.

Rafe ate his caterpillars, pulling them into his mouth with his lips, crunching them in his teeth, and licking the bark plate clean with his tongue.

The Indian women sat by their fire. One stitched a piece of cloth or leather, the other made a fish trap out of slender twigs, laying the thicker pieces in the fire for a moment before shaping them, then holding them until they were cool and kept their shape.

Then the sun had gone and darkness came down among the big trees.

Deerskin and Hareskin covered the fire over, making darkness darker. They went into the skin tent. It had a back and sides but no front. In there they sat and smoked pipes, now and then coming out to the fire to find a glowing coal to light up again with. On one of her journeys Deerskin pulled a fold of the tent over Rafe, and he began to feel warmer.

He slept again. He woke once, suddenly, out of a terrible

dream that he was tied up in the forest, and found that he was, but the real thing did not seem so bad as the dream. Inside the tent Deerskin sat and smoked. Hareskin was asleep.

The next time he woke because something had got hold of him. Something was on top of him, holding him down so that he could not move, covering his mouth so that he could not speak. This was of course worse than a dream, and worse than real. In the tent Hareskin and Deerskin were both asleep. Rafe thought that there were things in the forest he had not been told about, something stronger than animals, more frightening than ghosts.

He hoped that Deerskin or Hareskin would hear and wake. Then he thought they might be dead first, and he knew he would be in a moment.

The thing holding him down, covering his mouth, began to breathe against his ear. Where it breathes is where it keeps its teeth, thought Rafe. What is it? Can it be the mother of the caterpillars?

The breathing turned slowly into a word.

"Rayaf," it said. "Rayaf."

It was Tawena, the Indian girl. He stopped being frightened at once. He knew she had the knife and would rescue him. He relaxed, he stopped being a person under attack. He waited for her to get off him and turn him over, undo his thumbs, and lead him away, back to the village.

"Rayaf," she said again, and again, until she was sure he knew who it was. All his life Rafe would remember this dark night when his only friend came to visit him in the vast forest with danger close by. But at the time he was disappointed, because the girl only spoke to him. "Bear come," she said. "Tell Indian womans take you ever home. I tell bear tell Indian womans." And she said it five times, in different ways, so that he understood. Then she let his mouth go, and he had the sense not to speak. She

36

lifted herself away from him, and had gone. Hareskin and Deerskin still slept on. Rafe lay wondering what next would happen.

Tawena's plan of talking to the bear did not seem to work. The next thing that Rafe heard was a shriek not far away, Tawena's shriek of alarm.

Hareskin and Deerskin woke at once, sitting up, listening, in the darkness of the tent.

Somewhere in the woods beyond, behind them, there was more noise, louder shrieks, and screams. And with the screams came the growl of the bear, the great noise of it moving about, and something like the snapping of its teeth. There was a shout of pain, and then, echoing among the trees, a last scream from Tawena, stopping suddenly. Tawena's talk with the bear was over. In Rafe's head the noise stayed. It seemed to echo back from the distant trees.

There was a fearful crunching noise now. Rafe remembered how he had eaten whole caterpillars, and at this minute the bear was eating Tawena in the same way, straight with its teeth.

And now, he thought, the bear would not tell the Indian women anything, because it had not been told.

The Indian women stayed in their tent. Rafe did not know what they thought, but it seemed that they did not care. They let the bear finish its meal. After a time Rafe heard it walk off into the distance, and all was silent in the forest again.

Rafe slept. He had stopped being able to think, and his eyes closed by themselves. He was woken for a third time that night, this time by a deep and loud shouting from close by. He heard Hareskin and Deerskin get up, because the deep shout had words in it. The words came slowly out from the trees. Now and then among them was the snuffling noise of the bear. Rafe knew the sound well from

37

the fishermen's hut on the ice, the snuffing, sniffing, large breathing, and the noise of claws on wood. The bear had come back and was talking, telling them all something.

Deerskin and Hareskin were listening. They were attending and obeying; they were answering quietly. After all, the bear was telling them what Tawena said it would. Rafe knew now that the only way to tell the bear anything was to let it kill and eat you, and that was how Tawena had given it the message. She had died, she had been torn apart by a wild creature, just to save him, Rafe. He knew it must be so, though he did not understand a word the bear said.

All at once the bear had stopped speaking. It grunted once or twice more. In the tent Hareskin and Deerskin spoke to one another in a whisper. Out in the forest there was only great silence.

When daylight crept under the trees Deerskin came out and opened up the fire, keeping her face away from the smoke. Hareskin came out and stood over Rafe. She took the stone knife from her pouch and laid it in her hand. She bent down to him, pulling him up with the other hand.

Rafe could see again all that had happened during the night. He remembered how Tawena had come so close to him and held him down. He remembered, just as if it was happening again, how the bear had taken her. But now it seemed the bear had not understood the message; or perhaps Deerskin and Hareskin had not understood it, or did not want to obey.

Hareskin raised the stone knife in her right hand. It came closer and closer to Rafe. The Indian woman was ready to cut the skin off his head, Indian fashion, and tie his scalp to her belt.

six

The stone knife was in Hareskin's right hand. Her left hand came down on Rafe's shoulder and pulled him upright. As he stood there the knife came down behind him and cut the thong binding his thumbs together.

His arms were no longer tied. Rafe felt the knife had cut them off, because they were dead, as if they no longer belonged to him at all, though they hurt like his own. They ached and twinged. They did not like to be behind his back and fell forward to his side, but if he let them swing forward the pain grew horrible, as if his bones were being twisted; and if he tried to hold them back that hurt just as much. He wanted to hold his arms, but his hands could not be made to work. Something hammered in his thumbs.

He thought he would rather lose his hair, skin, and scalp.

All round him he heard the forest noises, and they hurt him too. He closed his eyes, because what he saw was uncomfortable. He stood still for a long time. After that he saw his hands in front of him, red and swollen, his thumbs ringed with the mark of being tied. They still felt like some other person's hands and would do nothing for him. Then the pain turned to pins and needles and a buzzing inside the hands and arms.

Deerskin gave him a push. While he had been standing and waiting for his arms she and Hareskin had folded up the skin tent, kicked down the fire, and were ready to move away.

Rafe walked where they sent him. Again Deerskin went ahead and Hareskin behind.

Rafe put one hand in the other. They could hardly bear to touch. Though they were in front and he could see them, he was sure they were behind him as well, as if they had set solid.

Hareskin grunted at him, but he did not know why. At least she had stopped making a knife and was not chipping away to make what could scalp him.

Rafe's arms would hurt all day, and all the next night. But at least he was alive. He wondered, as soon as they started walking, why something more dreadful had not happened to him. He remembered a sort of dream that something worse had happened to someone else. He remembered how Tawena had come to him, and what took place after that. Perhaps what she said had been true. And he wondered how it could have been.

Deerskin stopped. They had walked only a few yards from the camp. Rafe did not think they had reached any particular place: all the forest was alike to him, all trees with snow high up, all ground with snow below.

Deerskin was looking at the snow below, at the ground. Where she had stopped there was a trampled area, with large footprints and small, treading on one another, as if a large thing and a small thing had danced here.

40

Deerskin grunted. She put her hand down to measure a large footprint. That was where a bear had trodden. Rafe saw that, and knew that the other prints were from Tawena's much smaller foot.

This was not a place where anyone had danced.

This was the place where the bear had caught Tawena. In the middle of it there was a red mark on the snow, and two or three scraps of an old brown dress. Rafe knew it had not been a dream, that Tawena had come to him, then the bear had come to her, and that was all.

Deerskin said one or two words to Hareskin and moved on again. Rafe did not know whether he was sorry to leave or glad to have seen, to be sure what had happened. He knew he was alive, but he was not sure whether it was because of Tawena or not.

They walked on. Hareskin began to tell him something. He was doing what did not please her. He began to remember where he should put his feet: exactly where Deerskin had put hers. Hareskin put hers in the same place, and no one could tell how many Indians had passed that way.

All the morning under the trees they walked. All morning Rafe wondered whether they had come to the place where he would be killed and left. Indians did not love the white men who had come to their country.

All morning nothing happened. All morning they put one leg before another and walked in one track, as nearly as they could with him, thought Rafe.

There was morning and longer than morning. Rafe had had nothing to eat. He had been near fainting when his arms were undone and he was still in pain. Now his legs began to weary, because he had to lift each one to place it cleanly in the mark left by Deerskin, and they were walking fast, faster than he would have liked even if he could have put his feet anywhere he wanted. He longed to skip and jump as he liked, though he did not feel strong enough.

Towards the ending of the day they stopped, without any warning. Deerskin decided it was a good place, under a rocky cliff, not far from a still-frozen waterfall.

Rafe thought it was only a wild place, but he began to see how the camp was hidden and protected, safe under the cliff of rock, with tangled thorn bushes surrounding it so no one could creep up, and standing a little higher so that from inside you could see over the bushes. It must be a place the Indian women knew.

He thought a fire would be lit and they would sit round it and eat. He hoped so. That did not happen. The skin tent was dropped against the rock but not put up. Deerskin and Hareskin talked to each other, and then spoke to him, though he did not understand what they said, and they did not understand what he said. He could tell that they thought he was remarkably stupid, by the way they spoke. They then gave him two pieces of wood and made him sit down.

They said they were going hunting. He hoped it was quite clear what they meant. It could have meant that they were going away for a time and would then come back to eat him, but he did not think it was so.

They went away. Before they had gone the length of a room they were out of sight, and never could they be heard. They turned into invisible parts of the forest. Rafe sat where he was and became invisible too, and could not be heard. In fact he propped himself against the skin tent and went to sleep, arms still aching, legs stretched, feet feeling bruised.

He woke suddenly in twilight, alone in the world of forest. Not far away he heard a growl he knew, the noise of bear. He sniffed and thought he could smell it. He stood up, and there were hot blisters under his feet. But he stood and looked through the darkening trees. He had to move slowly. He saw small animals moving, walking in clear places, climbing the bark of trees; he heard them chat to one another, call from tree to tree. He heard the wings of birds brush the snowy branches. There was neither sight nor sound of Deerskin or Hareskin. Rafe wondered whether he had been left. And he realised that though he had been sitting among the forest snows he was not cold. He had learned to keep warm.

But he grew cold a moment later, when he heard the bear growl not far off. When he looked in that direction he thought he saw it; he certainly saw something move, brown and large behind a tree. And then, looking round in the falling light he saw where the bear had walked in the camp close to him, coming and going, the great prints of its feet. He wondered why he was not eaten or dead, and shivered.

All at once there was something close beside him. It was Deerskin. She carried a rabbit she had caught. She looked at Rafe, and examined the footprints of the bear. She did not seem afraid. Rafe thought that perhaps there was nothing to be afraid of. Perhaps the prints were not those of a bear.

Then Deerskin put the animal down and looked at Rafe. She was angry with him. She stared and she stared, and she stared him down, so that he looked at the ground, blushing. He had done something wrong and he did not know what it was.

Hareskin came back. She had dug out half a dozen mice and tied up the stems and roots of several plants. She came walking round the track of the bear, and she too looked with anger and contempt at Rafe.

She pushed him away, a push like a hit. She dropped her bundle of things to eat and knelt on the ground. She scraped at a place and uncovered the dark ashes of a hearth. From her pouch she brought out the stone knife and a pinch of tinder, and from her sleeve a hard small bar of iron, and began to make fire, little sparks that lodged in the tinder and made a glow that grew bigger and bigger as she blew at it. Between the puffs at the fire she told Rafe what she thought of him. Although he did not think it was fair, because he had not known what he had been told to do, Rafe felt ashamed and that he had been wicked. The fire should have been ready for them.

"And," said Deerskin, who was busy getting the rabbit skinned, "the bear might have eaten you, and then where should we be!" Of course, Rafe did not understand a word of what was said, but he knew what it meant.

With his hurt hands and his stinging feet he went about gathering wood. He was crying a bit because they were cross and he had done wrong, but he did not want anyone to know.

The fire grew tall. The meat was stuffed with leaves, and put to roast against the flame. The roots went into the few ashes as they were made. If he had lit the fire when they left there would be a heap of ash now, ready for cooking. They told him about it, and were not pleased with him.

However, when the cooking was done they gave him his share. His mouth was watering for it long before that, and his stomach growling and waiting. It was worth waiting for. The meat was tender and tasty with the leaves in it, the roots were warm and soft. After it they licked their fingers and the two women smoked pipes. They told him what was going to happen to him.

The bear had told them, they said. At first Rafe was very glad about that. Then he was not so sure. The bear had told them to take him out of the forest and to sell him to someone who would find him useful. Rafe knew that some Indians, and people in some other countries, had slaves. He understood very clearly that he was only being

44

kept to be sold as a slave, and that Deerskin and Hareskin were going to be rich because of it. The fire was covered with earth, the night came down over him, and he fell asleep, trying to think about the things he had been told, and trying not to as well.

seven

In the morning Rafe was more worried about being hungry than about being sold as a slave. After all, slaves go to places you can escape from, not like this deep dark forest with snow above, snow below, bears, angry women, and girls who steal knives.

Hungry or not, he had to walk with Deerskin and Hareskin, one in front of him, one behind. At first his legs ached from yesterday's walking, from having to lift his knees to get his feet into the places where Deerskin had trodden. He became used to that, and to the slight pain in his middle and to his thumbs, which still felt bruised.

Once again they walked a long way. Now and then Deerskin spoke to Hareskin, or Hareskin to Deerskin. Rafe wondered whether they were talking about slavery, or about hunting, or about where to camp. At first he thought he would like to stop walking, more than anything, and not worry about eating. Then he found that he was beginning to enjoy the walking, one leg after another, keeping warm, moving along under the trees, smelling the smells of the forest, different at different times. He began to forget all his problems, and started whistling.

It was a mistake. Both women turned on him at once. Hareskin thumped him on the back and he thought his ribs were knocked in, and Deerskin took hold of his face and squeezed it. The whistle went away to nothing. All round in the forest there was a great stillness that had not been there before. In front of him and behind him the Indian women walked very angrily.

When they stopped, in a flat place on a hillside, they were still angry with him. They dropped the skin tent and went away into the woods.

This time Rafe knew what he was meant to do. He was meant to light the fire. But that was impossible, because he had nothing to do it with. He looked round, thought, and searched for the place where fire had been made before. He found it, lined with black charcoal. Next he looked for a hard stone, and found several without any difficulty. But he had no tinder, and no iron. There was wet moss, and there was damp moss, but no dry moss, on trees or under rocks. There was no metal. Tawena had taken his knife.

"They won't be cross if I *can't* do it," he thought. But he thought as well that the Indian women would think he was lazy. Just to prove he was not lazy he banged a few stones together, but nothing happened except a bruised thumb.

He fell asleep again, just as he had the day before. This time, again, he woke suddenly. But he was not hearing the bear. He was smelling smoke. He opened his eyes carefully, expecting Hareskin to be looking at him with hard eyes, Deerskin to be looking with great contempt.

They were not here. The camp site was empty. But it had changed. In the fireplace a curl of smoke was standing.

At the bottom of the smoke there was a little fire, of course. How could there be? Rafe had knocked stones together at that place, and put damp moss there, but he thought he had made no sparks. And he did not think he had put small wood on the moss.

He thought it could not be a mystery, because there are no such things. He thought that Deerskin or Hareskin had come back and been secretly kind to him. Rafe was all at once very happy, because one of them must like him, and perhaps things would not be so bad after all. And he thought he would have a good whistle while no one was around to scold him.

While he whistled he gathered firewood. Suddenly he did not feel alone in the woods any more; he did not feel forgotten by people and remembered by bears.

He was still whistling when Deerskin and Hareskin came silently into the camping place. Hareskin thumped him on the back again, and Deerskin twisted his face, and that was the end of the whistle.

He looked at them and decided they could never be kind to him. And in a moment they were unkind again. Overhead a blue bird came down to a branch, then saw the three of them below and flew away again, giving a whistling call. This time Deerskin hit him on the shoulders and Hareskin pushed him in the face, thinking he had given the call.

Rafe gathered wood. He felt his eyes growing warm as if they wanted to cry. His chin wanted to wobble. But he did not let himself cry. He carried wood. He wanted to say several severe things to the Indian women, not knowing what they could be and whether they would understand; or whether his chin was strong enough to speak.

He sat by the fire, on a snowy stone. He helped cook the three birds the women had brought back, and put roots like parsnips to roast in the ashes. After that there was a sort of rough, bitter tea from a copper pot. The women gathered moss of certain kinds and dried it in their fingers by the glow of the fire. They handed Rafe some of his own to dry.

"This," they said, "is how to make tinder," though he did not know any of their words.

All at once the little group of them round the fire felt like a family. Rafe felt he belonged to them and they belonged to him. He was full of tough bird and woody parsnip, and they had been kind to him, and they were all three alone in the wild places. What nice faces they had, he thought, when they were not cross.

When his tinder was dry he took the two stones he had banged together when he was trying to light the fire, and showed how no sparks would come from them. Deerskin laughed at him. Hareskin looked at him in a funny way. She reached into her pouch and brought out the stone knife, which made Rafe stop smiling. She brought out some dry tinder and two pieces of iron. She gave one piece of iron to Rafe, and put the other away. She put away all her tinder.

She took up both of Rafe's useless stones and banged them together hard, but carefully. One of them split in two. She gave a half to Rafe. With that half and the piece of iron he was able to make sparks, able to catch them on his tinder, and to make fire. It was indeed how his mother made fire, but Mrs Considine had a new little box with all the things in.

The fire was covered over, and the last of the daylight dropped out of the sky. It was time to sleep again the deep sleep of night.

Before he slept Rafe heard the far howling of wolves. Deerskin and Hareskin murmured to one another, sitting in their tent and smoking. If the wolves came nearer, Rafe thought, the men of the village would go out and shoot them, because the white man was afraid of wolves. The Indian women were not alarmed at all.

The next day the walk continued at daylight. Rafe was used to being hungry as he walked, and did not mind it. In fact he thought it did not matter. He thought he might keep a breakfast bone tomorrow from tonight's meal. He walked steadily and never trod in the wrong place, and did not whistle though he felt like it. When they came to a stopping place he could have gone on for longer. Instead he lit the fire. It took him a great deal of time, and very much puffing and blowing, and there was not much fire ready when Deerskin and Hareskin came back, although they were away much longer than they had been on the two previous days.

They did not bring much with them: a small thing like a rabbit, a strong and peppery root, and a wooden toadstool that Rafe could not swallow. What he really wanted was a large chunk of bread, and perhaps some bacon fat, but there was nothing like that.

He went to bed hungry and woke hungry and then walked hungry the next day.

Day after day they went through the woods. One dusk, they walked to the edge of the woods and the lake was there in front of them. There was ice on its shore and snow on its banks, but all the water was clear of floes now. It was the same lake, the women said, more with their hands than with their mouths. Far away across it there was another shore. Hills lay close to the ground, with snow on them, and sunlight on the snow.

Rafe had learned some words, more to do with food and the direction of the wind and the size of the fire, and what birds were called, and bear. He could say one or two of them, but Deerskin and Hareskin always found out about things before he did, so he never had to. What they told him now he did not fully understand, because they did not

50

speak often. They were not always bound to be talking, like his mother.

They did not camp by the lake but deep in the woods again, so that their fire would not be seen. That night they had fish, Deerskin coming back very wet from the lake side. It was the only time Rafe knew where either of them went to hunt.

They went on, day by day again. They left the lake, with a long day's climb up a mountain until they were out in the cold air above the trees. They could have seen for miles but for the fallen clouds. They came down among the trees, but not before Hareskin had caught herself another white hare. They ate the hare, and rolled the skin in cold ashes to dry it and keep it.

By now Rafe was carrying things on his back as he walked. He had become strong and well, in spite of going without food on some days, or having only leaves on others. He could light a fire in a minute. One day he had noticed a striped squirrel before Deerskin or Hareskin and caught it with his hands and felt very pleased. But they told him to stop dancing about and making a noise. He had not after all been quite so clever as an Indian boy would have to be. They looked at the little dead animal with a sad disgust, and laid it on the ground. They would not eat it, they said; they must not. There were people who would, they said, but not us.

The forest grew thinner, the trees further apart. At night the wolves sang closer, now to one side, now to another. The Indian women disregarded them. One day Rafe thought he saw the grey shapes gliding among the trees, when he was alone and lighting the fire. He said nothing; but that night the wolves howled close by.

eight

The wolves went further away, night by night; or
Deerskin led Rafe and Hareskin away from the wolves.
Rafe tried to ask about it, but he did not know the word for
wolf. He had to gnash his teeth, give a growl and a howl,
and pad about on all fours.

Deerskin thought he was mad, when he went through
his display by the fire as she was cooking. She did not
waste words on him, but twisted his face again with her
hand. She had just been attending to a pair of plain grey
squirrels cooking on a stick, so her hand tasted good,
strong with wild onion.

Rafe, however, sat down and sulked. He thought
Deerskin was impolite and unkind, and that made him
cross. If his mother had done something like that to him
he would have stamped about the house until the roof
rattled, and slammed the door, and Mrs Considine would
have told him to wait until his Da came home and see how
he larrups you. But since he never did, and thinking about

home made him long for it, even for the bad bits, Rafe sulked all the more.

As he looked into the darkening forest a tear crawled out of one eye and ran down his right hand, and another ran, or jumped, from the other eye, landing between his knees on a leaf.

He began to have his idea then. It was an extremely foolish idea, he thought long afterwards, but once he had started on it he could not let it go.

He looked at the forest. At the beginning of this journey into slavery he had been thoroughly frightened by the dense woodland, and been scared and quivering, terrified and shivering, at the darkness going on for ever, with distant movement, distant sinister noise, unknown things living out in the darkness, animals, plants, birds, and perhaps things he did not, and could not, think about. And there were, of course, Indians.

After these days walking through woodland, and now that the woodland was not quite so thick, Rafe was no longer afraid. He understood most of the noises, or took no notice of them. He was sure the Indian women did the same. Even the wolves, like the banshees his mother would talk about at home in Ireland, were only part of another story, belonging to other people. No wolves had come near him. All they had done was sing. At the beginning they had not been there; they had come and gone. Tonight, for instance, he could hear nothing.

Well, perhaps there was a far-off sound of singing.

Rafe put off his idea for another night. Tomorrow he would do it. It was a good and simple idea, and he wondered why he had not had it before, though he was glad he had not, because until now he would have been afraid of being alone.

The simple idea was to leave the camp at night by himself, go back to the shore of the lake, and follow it round until he came to the other side, and on the other side would be the village. "And there," he thought, "I will slam a few doors."

When he had decided what to do, and when to do it, he let a cross tear in each eye run back under his eyelids without crying itself, and came to the camp fire.

"I shall be able to catch things," he said to himself. He repeated it out loud, knowing that Deerskin and Hareskin could not understand any of his words unless he used the Indian ones.

"Tomorrow night," he told them, "I shall go home."

Deerskin gave him a leg bone of the squirrel. It was a sort of kindness, but not much, because she had already chewed everything off it except some leathery strings at one end. Rafe tried it, and then put it down. Hareskin took it then, cracked it open carefully, and ate some pink jelly from the middle. She explained to him in her own language.

"They are nice to me," thought Rafe. "Perhaps I should stay." But the idea was stronger than the kindness, and he was sure he would go.

A day later he was ready. He had nothing to take with him. When he looked at his empty hands, the empty sheath where his knife should hang, and thought that he would be hungry in a day's time, he nearly gave up. The idea was strong, and seemed good, because any idea is a good thing to have. He went on having it, and ate his meal that evening with his knees trembling with excitement. It was roots tonight, with wooden centres that no one could eat. The food stuck inside his mouth and was hard to swallow.

After the meal the women sat and smoked. They spoke to him, but he did not know what they said. He thought it was probably about being a slave, being sold somewhere down the country. He did not know. He wanted to be honest now and tell them he was going that very night, going home, somehow, anyhow, by himself, even if they would not understand. But his mouth seemed unable to say words, either because it was nervous or because the roots had clogged it up.

A long time later, when a cold, distant light showed the tent pitched against a rock, when the fire was like a little dream under its turf, when the Indian women were nothing more than folds in the ground, Rafe stood up in the cold and stole away.

He was free at once. For the first time he was alone, and could go where he liked, any way he liked. He picked his way as quietly, as undisturbingly, as possible through the trees.

Somewhere a branch snapped. To one side some small feet ran on a tree; to the other side something spoke with a small voice once or twice; behind him a creature walked along a path and brushed aside branches and twigs. Ahead there was another noise, where something gurgled and rattled. Rafe knew it for water, because he had seen it earlier in the day, and had fetched water in the copper pot.

He came to it, and it glinted and breathed in the starry moonlight, coming in and out of an armour of ice. He knew it ran off to the right, and his common sense told him that it ran downhill towards the lake, and that if he followed it he would get there too.

He had thought something else, as well. He knew he was not such a careful walker as an Indian, and that they could follow his trail as easily as he could walk a road in the village. But he thought that if he walked in the water he would not leave a mark, because the water changes all the time. If he walked down the stream to the lake he would not leave a track, and would get to the place where he wanted to be.

The water was cold as pain. Now and then the frozen top

of it held him, then broke under his weight. Other times it did not break but made him slip, slide and roll over on a rock. He felt snow against his skin where his shirt tore.

When there was no more ice the water ran down plain and clean. Another stream came down from the right, and the water grew deeper and ran more slowly. Rafe walked knee-deep in it, and thought it was not so cold. But on either side the trees were hung with frost, and behind him and ahead the branches touched across.

Behind him something moved among those trees. Not fast, not perhaps following him. But maybe following him; always there, not coming any closer, and not being seen.

Ahead of Rafe there was more than starlight or the last of the moonlight. There was a wide sort of light, and the trees were not there. He saw sky, and the dawn, coming in over the lake, because he had come to the place where the stream and lake met.

Here he came out of the water, on the left side, and went into the woods, and walked on, as well as he could.

It was very hard going all day, rough country, with fallen wood, prickly bushes, heaped rocks, steep cliffs, marshy ground and always, always, when he stopped (which he often had to do on running out of breath or falling off a crag), always he heard behind him the thing that followed, followed, with never a breath of voice, never a glimpse, merely breaking its way through the forest after him.

Rafe made his way to the lake shore itself, and tried to walk along there. It was too steep, and the ground slid away at once into deep water. There was no little beach, as there was at the village, and as there had been each time Deerskin and Hareskin brought him to the lake. It was a slope of bare black rock with a gnarled tree root now and then, and black water below.

Rafe knew that he was not going along the lake at all,

that he had come no distance during the morning, during the afternoon. Time was going by and still there was no way to go without a track of some sort. He supposed that Deerskin had always followed a track she knew and could see, though he could not see it at all.

There was no way along the lake. Rafe looked forward, and all he saw in fading daylight was headland after headland of black sharp cliff, with no way at the foot and no way at the crest.

His only companion was the thing that followed, louder, closer now, in the twilight.

He knew then that the idea he was following was a foolish one, and that he should never have started, and that even if he could go back the way he had come (and how could he do that with the follower in the track he made?), if he could retrace his steps, if he knew where to leave the stream he had followed down, even then the Indian women would have moved away, and there would be no one to find, no one to find him.

He sat against a tree in the cold dusk and wished he was dead already. He knew he soon would be. He wanted at least to go home and tell his mother what had happened, because she would want to know. But of course if he were at home he would not be here too.

Darkness came across the lake; darkness and a flurry of snow. The only good thing was that now he had stopped walking so had the follower.

Then he was in a shivery doze, dreaming he was warm, and waking was not; dreaming he ate and waking had not; dreaming he was with company and waking they had fled into silence.

Waking out of something that was not a dream he knew he had heard a movement. Before he could think anything more about that he truly heard the breathing in of a wolf about to snarl, then close against him the snarl itself, and following the snarl a great growl, on the end of that a howl close against his ear, and something touching his back and his side.

With that he was up and moving before he was awake, not knowing where he was going, not caring. The ground he trod on was not there, the place he escaped to did not exist. He fell, fell down the dark slopes of the shore towards the water, and behind him the howl of the wolf turned to another noise, of some beast he could not think of and would never know, and that beast laughed with a ringing laughter, and its noise echoed among the trees and over the lake.

In the darkness, as he fell and ran, ran and fell down the slope, something in his path took hold of him, wrapped itself round him, and held tight. In the darkness the great laughing stopped.

nine

The thing holding Rafe laughed quietly. He struggled and tried to get away, but it had wrapped his arms to his side.

There was some other creature making a roaring and howling noise, and Rafe wanted to get away from that as fast as he could. It seemed to him that the new roaring and howling noise was a bigger danger than the thing that had hold of him already.

The thing that held him put a paw on his mouth. At that moment the roaring stopped. Rafe naturally tried to bite the paw across his mouth. It stopped being a paw and became a hand, a hand that did something it had often done before. It twisted his face, though not very hard.

It was the hand of Deerskin. It was Deerskin who had hold of him, Deerskin who had prevented him from falling into the lake. He could see its deep clear water below them both now, with the morning coming up beyond the forest the far side. He could see Deerskin.

The roaring he had heard was not the wolf close behind

him. It had come from his own mouth. The paw, Deerskin's hand, had stopped the noise.

"Sagastao," said Hareskin, coming down the hillside, laughing again, laughing at Rafe. In the middle of the laughing she gave a small wolfy howl, to show that she had been the wolf that woke him up, and to remind him of the time he had made noises like that.

"Sagastao," she said again, and pointed with her lips at the dawn coming up.

Rafe had stopped struggling by now. He was so glad to be rescued that he clung on to Deerskin, hugging her, holding her, as if she were the only safe place in the whole world. She and Hareskin had followed and saved his life. They had come straight to him. He thought that was marvellous, because he had left no track when he waded through the water; no track and no scent.

Deerskin took his arms from round her, gently, kindly. She lifted up his head and looked into his eyes. Rafe did not know how he looked, but he thought it would be wild. He could feel that his mouth was open, his neck stiff, his throat tight.

Deerskin put both her hands on his face and gave it a twist without actually twisting it at all, so that nothing hurt, though he knew what had been done. It was like an imitation smack from his own mother.

It did not hurt his face at all. It hurt him all the way through and inside, so that he knew how badly he had behaved, how he had been so ill-mannered, so ungrateful, how he had insulted the people who had kept him alive, how he had scorned their feelings, wasted their time and annoyed them. What they had done was follow him patiently, creep up on him in the dark, and give him a very great fright. They thought it was funny, and somehow so did Rafe.

So he laughed, and he cried, and he wept and spluttered

and his nose ran and his legs gave way and his sides hurt
and he could not breathe, until at last Hareskin came and
picked him up, shaking him so that all the laughter and
giggle and silliness fell out of his head, and brought him to
a fire she had made, where there was a fish to be eaten.

It was like being home again, warm and fed, with friends
and closer than friends: like mother and sister.

After the fish the fire was put out and they walked back
those few miles to the camp Rafe had left.

They showed him his track from where they had found
him to the edge of the stream. He could not believe he had
broken such an ugly way through. He did not remember
breaking branches down like that, or tearing the bark so
that white wood showed. But there the trail was, as if an ox
and cart had come through.

He did not want to walk in the stream again, and he did
not have to. He was puzzled when Hareskin showed him
the track they had followed, along the bank all the way,
because he had not come along the bank. Yet here was his
track, and there were the marks of his boots in snow and
clay, a little melted, but still clear.

"I did not do it," he said. Deerskin looked at him as if he
were without hope of being anything more than a clumsy
bear, and Hareskin prodded him in the back, as usual, to
make him walk tidily now.

At the old camp something had eaten what had been
there, but another meal, of fish and meat, brought up from
the lake, was cooked. Rafe had room for it. Then, sitting by
the fire, he saw lights began to twinkle in his eyes. He fell
over, asleep. He felt Hareskin taking his boots off his feet,
and the dampness going from his toes when the firelight
warmed them. He lay like a fallen tree until the next
dawn.

When he woke the whole of the idea had gone from his
mind. It had not worked out at all well, but he was happier

now that he had done it, happier to be with the Indian women, than he had been before.

Who knows what ideas do? He went to gather wood for the fire.

In the day or two that followed they did not move far. They spent a day among some rocks while Deerskin and Hareskin listened. They were being cautious about something they heard or scented and wanted to avoid. Rafe did not know what it was, but waited with them, staying with one while the other went away to scout. He learnt how to make the meshes of a fishnet from the long fibres of a creeper.

After the middle of the day Hareskin went to listen, look and perhaps hunt. Both women were uncertain about what was going on somewhere in the forest, and were very uneasy. While Hareskin was gone Deerskin took a shaped slender stick from among her things and bent it carefully between her hands. Then she hung a string from one end, quite a short string, sinewy, curly, and handed the thing to Rafe.

He did not know what it was. The string was in a notch at one end of the stick. There was a similar notch at the other end, but the string was not long enough to reach it, and if it did there would be no use in it.

"I am being stupid," said Rafe, out loud.

"Monyas," said Deerskin, meaning that he did not know very much at all. It made him think.

What was the thing? He bent the wood a little, as Deerskin had done. She watched him and said nothing. He had done nothing wrong. He bent it a little more. That was not wrong either.

Then he saw what the thing was, how the wood was the bow and the string the cord that drove the arrow. He bent the wood more and brought the cord across, little by little, to the notch.

"Tapwa," said Deerskin, and watched him miss the first attempt to get the cord in the notch, and have the stick unfold and knock the breath from him.

The second time he almost got it, and managed not to be winded. The third time the thing completed itself in his hands. It was no longer some wood and some sinewy cord, but a living, vibrating, tense thing, with a feeling of its own life inside it.

Deerskin brought out an arrow. She took the bow in her right hand, the arrow in her left, held the bow across in front of her, her left hand to the string, putting the arrow against it and against the wood, and with a sudden quiet pull letting the arrow go, and it hung against the bark of a tree.

Rafe ran for it and pulled it down. It had held itself in a crack, not having hit very hard. It had a small blunt point of stone, the size of Rafe's thumb nail, shaped, gummed, tied.

"For birds," said Deerskin, in words and signs. "Bring bird down. This is a woman's bow. Men have a bigger one. But you are a child and must use a woman's bow. A man will use a woman's bow in the thick forest." She gave him bow and arrow.

He tried slowly to fit them together, to make them come to the right state, to be fired and hit what he wanted to hit.

Deerskin would not let him do it that way. She wanted him to do it quickly, not slowly. She wanted him to learn it quickly from the beginning. He could understand what she meant, but not her explanation of it.

At the beginning the arrow fell from his hand before he had it to the string. He could tell that Deerskin was being patient with him, that she thought he was a very long way worse than any Indian boy would have been. Gradually arrow came to bow, and slowly bow came up to be fired, and at last he drove an arrow several feet into the air and

63

was able to go to fetch it. He practised with an arrow that had a burnt point, not a stone head that had to be patiently made and would be spoilt by one use.

When Deerskin thought he had done enough she made him take the cord from the bow, roll it up and put it in a pouch made for it. She tucked it, the arrow, and bow away. She sent him for firewood.

When they had the wood they waited, waited, for Hareskin, while it grew a little darker among the rocks, the sky greyer, the air colder. And still there was no fire.

Far away there was a sound, one single sound. Rafe was on his feet as soon as he heard it. A rifle had cracked its report into the air a mile, two miles, away, and the echo of it, or perhaps only the memory of it, came from tree and cloud, rock and lake, after the first fierce blow.

Much more than an hour later Hareskin came quietly back to them, her brown eyes looking large in the twilight, different from usual. Deerskin spoke to her, and put up the tent. They were to stay here tonight, Rafe understood, and he was told to light the fire. Hareskin had brought back a deer, and they were to eat that. Rafe looked at it, and knew how to cook it. "I am learning things," he said. "I know what to do." And he asked for the stone knife and skinned the deer, while the fire built up red coals. He sensed something was wrong.

Hareskin sat by the fire and watched. When the meat was cooked she did not eat any. She sat with her arms folded and her eyes large, saying nothing.

Rafe grew unhappy about her. She was not as she should be, not as she usually was. Tonight she was doing nothing at all, not helping, not correcting, not eating. He touched her elbow, because he did not like her to be so still, like a bow without the cord.

She looked at him and still said nothing. Her breath came slowly and shudderingly. She was pale, and by the

64

light of the fire Rafe saw sweat on her face. He remembered what his mother had said, when someone was hurt in the village (one of the men had died), that a pale face and sweat meant trouble.

Then Hareskin fell over where she sat, and moaned. Her arms came unclasped, and from her left shoulder there ran blood, dark in the firelight, the blood coming from a great hole at the top of her arm, and in the hole something that glittered.

It was the bullet that had flown from the rifle they had heard, and while Deerskin and Rafe had heard only that and the echo, Hareskin had caught the bullet, and brought that back so that they all now knew about the gun.

"Is she dead?" said Rafe, not wanting to know, not wanting to hear how his friend was hurt.

ten

That night Rafe's own shoulder ached, ached and hurt. He could feel in his mind, and then in his shoulder, the pain Hareskin must have, with a hole in the top of her arm, and in the hole the crooked, hot remains of a metal bullet.

So he woke and slept, and the night seemed long. He thought Deerskin did not sleep at all. He saw her often beside the little fire, in the frosty mist among the trees laying sticks on the small glow, twice using the copper basin to make tea.

Rafe offered once to come and sit beside the fire with her, but she waved him away with her elbow. Behind her, in the tent, Hareskin moved a little, and as she did she woke the pain and drew in her breath.

Deerskin woke him before full daylight, when the sun was still coming up the tree trunks, and fans of shadow from tree branches lay across the mist, where still the rocks among the trees had huge black holes of shadow at their backs.

Deerskin's face was cold, grim, alien, when she sent Rafe to gather wood for the fire. He went without a word. He was cold too, after being in the warm fold of the tent all night. He wanted to run and bring warmth into his legs and hands. But he knew better than that now. He walked as quietly and tidily as he could, careful where he trod, knowing that he could not be doing it anything like so well as an Indian. He gathered wood with great care, too, lifting pieces and leaving no trace of what he had done.

When he had a bundle under one arm and a branch under the other (making sure he did not let the twigs trail on the ground), he stood for a moment and looked up the sunshine into the forest, where the distance turned white with sun on mist, and looked down the sunshine into the sun, where the tree trunks were black against the red fire. He realised that he was alone again, as he had been when he ran away. Then he had not known what to expect and it had all been new. Now he could remember the last time, and how miserable he had been. And he had a dreadful feeling that it was happening again in a different way.

He remembered Deerskin's unkind, uncaring face when she sent him for wood. He thought that she wanted him out of the way, not just for a time, not even to bring wood, but for ever. He was sure that when he came back to the camp he would find the fire out, the tent gone, and the two women vanished, suddenly hurrying back to their own people, leaving the clumsy white boy who would never even make a good slave, leaving him to die alone.

The thought was terrifying, because now he knew what it was like to be lost, to be hopeless, to spend the night alone already dying of hunger, not able to catch anything. The thought was so terrifying that he at once had no idea where he was, which way he had come, how to get back and find out whether he was right or not. He had come along so neatly that he could not tell where he had been.

He just knew that he had come along with the sun on his left side, so he should go back with it on his right.

He set off, sure he had come by the rock that looked like a house. But he had not gone far towards it before it looked like a giant plum pudding in its square of cloth, and in a little while longer it was like the front of the ship he and his parents had come to the country in.

Rafe changed direction a bit, not being at all certain now about the rock. It altered too much. But when he started to walk a different path he was more lost than ever. A piece of branch under his arm snapped off suddenly and rattled down to the ground. Rafe turned round to look at it, thinking that something had jumped on him. He left it and walked on. Now there were two rocks close together, and he was sure he had walked between them. But when he came to them he found a thorny bush growing there, so that was wrong. He walked on. All at once he found the sun the wrong side of him, on the left, and turned round. He came across the piece of branch that had fallen off a quarter of an hour before.

Until then he had hoped he would be lucky, that he would strike the path. Now he knew he would not be lucky, could never find his way, should not have come so far from camp.

Out in the mist something coughed. Something moved. Something large broke branches. The cough, the movement, the breaking, were all the actions of a bear. All of Rafe's skin crinkled and became tight on him. His mouth turned dry and he wanted to swallow but had a stopped-up throat. His legs wanted to walk but he did not know where, and they did not know how.

The bear growled. This time Rafe moved. He wanted to drop the wood and run, but he could not make his arms and legs obey him.

He walked, quietly, so that the bear did not hear him. He

68

walked quite a long way. He was just as lost, though the bear was further away, he was sure. He thought he heard it far off, but there were birds, too, and other creatures moving about. They were at home; they were not lost.

The bear moved again, close by, with a snarly growl. Rafe moved away, and again he thought he had escaped from it, without getting anywhere. And a third time the bear came close and moved him on.

This time not all the mist moving round him was forest mist. This time he could smell smoke on it. He was near the camp, he knew, and in a very little while he was there. The fire burnt, Deerskin sat against it, and in the tent, which was still there too, Hareskin lay huddled.

"Bear," said Rafe, making Deerskin understand what he meant. She stepped away a little, and listened. Then she made it quite plain to Rafe that there was no bear near, had not been, and would not be, and that he was to stop being silly and fetch more wood.

Before he went he looked at Hareskin. She lay without moving on her side, her right hand across her left shoulder. Under its fingers the shoulder was swollen and hot. Her face was grey and covered with lines, as if she had been draped in a spider's web. Her eyes were large, large and very frightened and hurt. Rafe did not know what he could do, how he could help. He touched her face, but she did not care for that, though she knew it was the act of a friend. She lifted her head away and blinked at him.

Rafe fetched wood. He did not think where he was going, whether he was lost, how to get back, and had no difficulty at all. There was now no bear.

When he came back nothing had changed. He was sure something should have been done.

Deerskin had thought the same thing. She knew what had to be done, but it seemed it had been difficult to persuade Hareskin. Hareskin was in so much pain that nothing could be worse, anything must be better. Deerskin was waiting with her, and told Rafe to come across and help.

Rafe understood what was happening. The bullet in the wound had to come out. Deerskin had to act roughly and quickly, but it was the best way, Rafe thought. His father often said, "Strike while the iron is hot," and his mother said that what was done now was done soonest.

Deerskin took Hareskin's right hand away from the wound and gave it to Rafe to hold, wrapping his arms round it. Hareskin was about to say a word, but Deerskin did not give her the chance. Before anyone knew what was going on Deerskin sat on Hareskin, right on the bad arm and right across her, and had her fingers in the wound, pulling at the bullet in there.

Hareskin gave a short, sharp shriek, and went quite limp. Her eyes almost closed, her head dropped to one side. Rafe felt the arm he was holding grow soft, and he was sure she had died. But Deerskin did not stop. She was pulling at the bullet, which did not come easily away. Rafe looked and felt the crawling of his own nerves, as if they were being pulled out too.

Deerskin said, "Tapwa," which meant something was happening. The bullet came out and was thrown on the ground, jagged and torn, glittering with metal and shiny with Hareskin's blood.

Rafe felt a horrible coldness and darkness coming on him, and he fainted away. When he woke Hareskin was sitting up, Deerskin was beside the fire, and they were talking together. There was tea to drink, and they sat all three by the fire for a long time. Hareskin had pain, but not enough to complain about, and her face was not grey any more, though still pale. Rafe felt more shaken, he thought. And gradually hungry too.

Deerskin went out hunting, leaving him to care for

Hareskin. She was gone a long time, coming home as a blue evening settled among the rocks and trees, bringing four birds, a tangle of thin roots and a pocket of nuts.

The next morning the wound was closed, Hareskin was able to walk, and it was time to move camp. They set off as usual, with Deerskin in front, Rafe next, and Hareskin following.

The firm path under the trees grew soft, with water where feet had stepped. Rafe's boots went through the marshy ground, the spongy green moss underfoot sinking and quaking as he went. Water came in, because the boots were wearing through. He looked back to Hareskin and saw her walking in a stiff but swaying way on the uneasy ground. He knew it was the way white women walked, like his mother's own manner of going, and laughed quietly. He was not laughing at Hareskin; he was not laughing at his mother: it was out of some glad feeling that since everything was going well here, so it was at home; and Rafe felt his place was in both. He remembered one and saw the other, and found them much the same: if anything, perhaps the Indian women were easier to get on with than his mother was.

Rafe was better now at following, so he did not stay close to Deerskin, and Hareskin did not stay close to him. When he realised that Hareskin had been out of sight and hearing for a long time Rafe waited for her. She did not come up to him. He stood where he was. He wondered, again, whether they had arranged to step aside from the way and leave him alone. But for the time being he waited where he was, in a pleasant place, with the sun coming and going high up among little clouds.

Deerskin came back to him and went past, down the way they had come. Rafe followed.

They came to Hareskin, who sat against a tree, her face red and large, swollen with some poisoned fever, and her shoulder the same, festered, throbbing, red, the rest of her arm blue and pale, with redness running along it.

Worse than that, Hareskin did not know that Deerskin was there, that Rafe was there. She looked at, and spoke to, people who were not in the forest with her.

Deerskin went off with the copper basin and brought cool water, putting that on her face and on the shoulder. Rafe sat down and thought. Then he lit a fire. Deerskin did not want a fire, but Rafe told her quite plainly, in English, that there was going to be a fire. He knew what had to be done.

He had seen his mother deal with such swollen wounds. He knew the treatment was not dribbles of cold water, because that could do nothing to help.

When the fire was going well he told Deerskin to look after it, which was quite the other way from usual, when she told him to do things. Then he went back down the track a little way, to where he had seen what he wanted, in the marshy ground beyond the stream.

Here he gathered the green of a growing moss, bringing back an armful of the wet stuff, torn from the ground. As he came back he picked out the hard stems, the sharp pieces, and ended with a soft bundle. All its wetness ran down his clothes, but he did not care.

At the fire Hareskin still sat against the tree. Deerskin still bathed the closed wound. Rafe took away the copper basin of water. Next he took off his shirt, then got his teeth into it and ripped a whole sleeve from it. He took a pad of moss and filled the middle of the sleeve, rolling the whole sleeve up, and then wrapped the rest of the shirt round it, and put the part full of moss in the copper basin. He set the basin on the fire, and boiled the shirt and the moss. Deerskin picked up a strand of the remaining moss and tasted it. She did not think much of it.

Rafe lifted the basin from the fire with two pieces of

wood, and took the shirt from the water. Not all the shirt had gone in, so there were two ends, one the collar, the other the shirt-tail, still dry (but a little scorched).

He held these ends, and boiling water dripped from the middle, steaming on the fire. He twisted the ends, and squeezed water from the middle, where the moss was, squeezed as hard as he could, until there was only a dry, steamy hotness. He pulled out the whole sleeve, with the moss inside, feeling it with his hand, so that it was not too hot.

He had made a hot poultice, knowing that was the right treatment. Deerskin watched him. He laid the hot thing on Hareskin's shoulder and tied it there, pulling the other sleeve from his shirt to make a bandage. Hareskin lay still, feeling nothing, very ill.

"Hmn," said Deerskin, deep in her throat and doing nothing to interfere. She went to fetch more water.

They camped there. That night there was nothing to eat, but Deerskin set traps down in the stream. They camped against the tree where Hareskin sat. Twice more in the day, and three times in the night, Rafe made fresh poultices and put them on, and twice on her own Deerskin did the same, while he slept.

In the morning Hareskin was no better, hot and stiff. Rafe ate fish that Deerskin brought, unable to taste it or enjoy it. Hareskin would eat nothing, only drink water.

They stayed in that camp. Towards the middle of the day Hareskin's eyes closed. She was dying, Rafe thought. But he made her another poultice, though all they had given her so far had done nothing. But cold water would have been worse than nothing. It came to Rafe's mind that if Hareskin died, Deerskin would bury her, or lay her high in a tree, and go home, leaving him to die alone.

Some time later, when the sun had gone down just its own width from its highest place, Hareskin opened her eyes, opened her mouth, and spoke. Rafe did not know the words, but Deerskin did, and went to her. Rafe could not tell whether sadness or relief was in her voice, but something more than words was there. Deerskin lifted off Rafe's last poultice, though it had not been long there. She took it away into the forest. Rafe looked at Hareskin. Hareskin looked at him. She smiled, as much as she ever did, and he knew the poultice had worked. He knew it had drawn the poison out of the wound.

Deerskin came back without Rafe's shirt-sleeve. She said, in her own language, but he knew what she meant, that the bad stuff had come from Hareskin's shoulder, and that the poultice had done it.

Rafe put another poultice on Hareskin, because she was not cured yet. He was the doctor now, and they did as he said.

That night Hareskin ate fish and drank a great deal of tea.

Before Rafe went to sleep Deerskin came to him and took his face in both her hands, as if she might give it the greatest twisting in the world, and spoke to him. He did not know what she said, but they were good words, good words from a kindly face. As good, nearly, as a mother, Rafe thought, and slept.

That night, as he lay asleep, something came close to him and stood there, and he woke knowing it was there. Then it lay against his back, and he dared not move, and hardly breathed, with the wild warm thing pressed against him in the dark. And not far away, the wolves ran again about the forest.

eleven

In the morning the thing had gone from beside Rafe. In fact he had slipped back to sleep while it was still there, and at daylight had to be woken by Deerskin, who said to him, "Rayaf, Rayaf," just like Tawena saying his name.

He decided that the thing in the night had been only a dream. But Deerskin found marks on the ground and followed them away from the camp, looking and talking and puzzling over what she saw. She could not tell Rafe what she had seen.

That day Hareskin had poultices again. The fever left her, the swelling went down, and she moved her arm again. She ate. She walked about, she spoke. In the evening of that day's rest she gathered firewood with Rafe, and at night smoked her pipe. Her eyes were no longer too big, no longer dull. Before she slept she combed out her hair. Rafe put on a shirt with no sleeves.

The walking began again next day. They had not gone far, perhaps a mile, when Deerskin stopped at a footprint in the snow, bigger than the print of a bear. She said something to Hareskin and they looked with care at that print and others leading to it and away. Even Rafe knew these were not the tracks of a white man, and were more than a day old. Something big had made them, but nothing so big had lain next to him. Deerskin led on, and Rafe followed, his feet where hers had been, leaving the marks behind.

The lake appeared on their right again. There was sunshine and soft snow. Rafe saw the far shore of the lake, closer now, with the hills standing high over the water, snow streaked with dark where rock showed through. In the snow where he walked, each time he put his foot down there was damp at the bottom of the print.

The sun went behind clouds and there was misty rain. The hills beyond the lake went out of sight, scribbled out by the drizzle.

He saw them again a few days later, when they walked away from the water and at last back to it again.

These many miles further on, the far side of the lake had come closer. It was close enough for him to see the shore itself, not just hill tops. He could see the trees marching to the water and standing at its edge, green with the snow melted from them, and birds overhead. On the lake itself the arrows of wild geese and duck came flying in, feeding in shallow places where the reeds and rushes grew like grass through the water.

They ate goose and fresh leaves at night now; roasted duck, the eggs of wild forest birds. Rafe learned the Indian words for many things, most of them with no English name that he knew.

The Indian women were pleased with him for that. They were not pleased about another thing, and thought him very stupid. In the snow it had been easy for him to put his feet where Deerskin had walked. Now they

76

crossed large areas where no snow remained he often could not see where Deerskin had walked. Deerskin and Hareskin could see things like that very well, and Rafe had to learn it too. At first Hareskin would grunt at him when he stepped in the wrong place. When he did not get better she would tap him with a stick. When she started to do that Rafe made a fuss, and when he did Deerskin turned round and pulled his face in that very painful way.

He learned how to see faint dry marks on faint dry rock, and to put his foot there. But now and then it was impossible. Hareskin would push him and sniff to tell him how he should have known by smell. And they would both wave their hands about to show how Rafe was worthless.

He thought they meant he would not make a good slave, when he came to be sold. He did not want to be a slave, and did not mind what they thought about that. Then he thought that if he was worthless they might leave him alone in the middle of the forest, and if he could not track things and see what was there he would die. So he taught himself to see the smaller signs.

Day by day he grew better. But every day he found something more he had not seen, things so plain that he ought not to have missed them. In the broad leaves of a clump of bushes in a little valley, away from big trees, were some small grubs that tasted of honey. They had an extra meal of those; but Rafe had not seen them at all, and if he had he would not have thought about eating them. It was not fair, he thought, that he was expected to know as well as see.

He heard, however, night after night the wolves running by the lake side. One day, in a thick fog, Deerskin went further ahead than usual, and out of sight. That did not matter, now that Rafe could follow so well. But behind him Hareskin followed slowly too, because she did not

77

need to stay close and correct him. When Rafe looked back he thought he saw her shape in the swirls of fog. When he looked forward he saw ahead of him a grey shape that was not Deerskin. The shape stopped moving and looked at him. It was a grey timber wolf, following its own track and crossing Deerskin's, stopping a moment to know the strange scent.

The wolf looked into his eyes and moved on. Rafe did not stop walking. For a moment he had been too startled to do anything except what he was already doing, and then it was too late to stop. When he came to the place where the wolf had crossed he smelt on the air that iron scent of wolf.

Behind him the wolf turned to follow again, one wolf and then a second, sniffing his track. Then behind them again was Hareskin, and the wolves turned aside.

The lake stopped being a lake. It became a wide river, sometimes singing down between rock cliffs, sometimes tumbling and thundering over boulders and rapids, bright with yellow clay, clearing the winter out of the northland. They walked beside its noise several days, in clear open country where walking was easy on grass, but there was little to eat.

Then they cut across a hill away from the water. On the far side of the hill the ground began to shake, a small vibration like the one Rafe had often felt from rolling a marble or a bullet down a rough plank. Ahead of them there was cloud on the land. Then, all at once, the hillside stopped and a cliff fell down towards the river, and down the cliff the river ran in a huge waterfall, as wide as the water, higher than many houses, higher than many trees, the river leaping off the mountain and digging its way into the ground before running to the lake.

They were to cross the river at the fall. Rafe thought it would be the worst and wildest place to do it, with the water pounding and pouring close beside them. They went down to the very edge of the falling water, and there, against the mountain, there was a gap behind the water, where a narrow ledge ran round behind. Here Deerskin led the way, and Rafe had to follow. Deerskin seemed very small against all the water. Even the drops were as big as her head.

Then they were all three behind the moving curtain that was falling and falling for ever, letting a brown light through, hurtling and hurling itself past so heavy and relentless, making more noise than Rafe had ever known. Now and then a greater noise plunged past when a slab of rock came down the water, faster perhaps than anything so large could move. It was as if ten million horses ran down the mountain with their hooves drumming all the way.

At the back of the water the small figure of Deerskin picked a slippery path through cold spray, holding on to rocks, resting each foot against something firm, moving with caution. Anyone could tell, even if he had not the wild senses of an Indian, that if the water took hold of you, if you fell over that edge into it, that was the last thing you would know.

Slowly, slowly, they went through that place. Not once, not twice, but seven times, the ground seemed to give under Deerskin, and seven times she found a firm footing and saved herself.

At last, when Rafe was getting so cold and wet he thought he might not be able to hold on any longer, the light grew brighter, the hanging water grew less thick, the path flattened, and Deerskin was out on the cliff face, with the fall behind her.

Rafe looked back to Hareskin. She came along as best she could. None of them followed footprints, because they were washed away as soon as they were made. Beyond Hareskin Rafe thought he saw a grey wolf picking its way behind the fall on four legs, like Rafe himself. But then he was out of the water and following Deerskin along a ledge.

Deerskin stopped, and Rafe caught up with her. She had stopped because on the ledge ahead of her was the bear again, walking towards them in a narrow way where there was no room to pass.

Hareskin came along the path to join them. It was the only place they could walk on, with cliff above and cliff below, with the wetness of the fall still showering them and making mud of the surface, and the thundering of it making the ground quiver, and the roaring of it taking away all the sound so that the bear had not heard them, and the wind running up the water so that it had not smelt them.

Hareskin signalled that they should turn back, cross the river again, and try another day. Deerskin considered what to do. There was time still, because the bear was looking round, doing its own considering.

Rafe thought about things too. First of all he wanted to be doing something brave, like dealing with the bear in front of the Indian women, because they had saved his life over many days, even if they were taking him to be a slave. However, he had no idea how to deal with a bear, except for a certain feeling that you do not try.

He had another feeling about it too, because there had been bears all round them, right from the day he and Tawena went to look at one. That bear had only wanted a lump of bacon to eat; in the forest a bear had looked at him without harming him; its tracks had come near but never threatened them. Rafe began to feel there was something different about bears, as Tawena had said. And it was plain that Deerskin and Hareskin were not going to fight. They only wanted to go along the path without bothering anyone. They thought of the bear as equal, but awkward.

Perhaps this bear was different. At last it saw them. It

looked hard, lifted on its hind legs, with a great claw to steady itself against the rock cliff. It snarled in a nasty way. Rafe thought they should turn and go. When he looked back, though, he thought he saw the grey wolf at the edge of the waterfall, on the same path. The bear snarled again.

twelve

A long time seemed to pass. The waterfall went on shouting its great shout. The sun came out for a little while and rainbows stood in the spray. Deerskin sat down in the path on a wet mossy rock. Rafe could not tell what she was thinking. He hoped she would do something of a large brave kind, like going to the bear and twisting its face, just as she twisted Rafe's for him when he was particularly stupid. Hareskin stood in the falling spray of the waterfall and Rafe did not know what she was thinking either.

In fact, he could hardly tell what he was thinking himself, because of the way the river roared against his ears, blocking out every sound from outside, and swallowing up all those inside. There was so much noise he had to look to see that he was there at all.

The bear came down on all fours. It had a look backwards to see whether it wanted to go that way, and decided it would not and probably could not. It looked up and saw there was no way there. Rafe thought that it could climb up the cliff if it had good intentions. It looked down, and went on thinking about going that way.

Rafe looked up and down too, and behind him again. There was no wolf to be seen now, no grey shape against the waterfall. There was nothing but the fall, the cliff, and the small water-cave that led to the far side.

Rafe heard rocks falling and breaking in the valley below. All at once his ears had grown used to the sound of the water, because it went on steadily all the time. Now he heard other sounds, as if the water had stopped flowing near him, leaving a little silence.

He heard the bear give a grunting growl. He heard Hareskin speak to Deerskin over his head. He wondered whether they had been talking all the time. He heard his own feet move on the path, and so did Hareskin, giving him a push to make him keep still. He always had to put his feet only where Deerskin put hers.

He heard a rock tumble away from under the bear's hind leg and thump down a slope of cliff and go over a steeper edge.

Away down the cliff he heard an animal move, heard it call, without being able to see it.

"Bear," said Hareskin, using an Indian word that he knew now. "Bear down below."

The bear heard as well, and gave an answering call. It now forgot about Rafe and the Indian women. It was not interested in going along the path any more, but it was a long long time before it decided to go somewhere else, as if it were not quite certain about its friend. It put a foot down on the slope. A second foot scraped a hold. The bear slithered down to the steep edge, paraded about on that, then tumbled over it like a sack, untidily, out of sight.

Later that night, when they were beyond hearing the fall, after they had walked themselves dry, and had only to be aired by the fire, when they had eaten a sort of hot fish jelly scooped from a stream, when the fire was low and the Indian women had smoked their pipes and gone to sleep, there was a noise again.

It woke Rafe before he heard it, a feeling in the ground before it came to his ear. There was a shake and a tremble, not very great, but more solid than the quivering of the ground near the waterfall.

Rafe sat up. The women were awake, speaking to one another. Now Rafe heard what they heard, the noise on the air. Once at home, before he and his parents came to this country, the house chimney had taken fire, putting up a large plume of scorched smoke. The fire had climbed the inside of the chimney, biting and roaring as it went, pulling air in at the grate, jetting fire and fumes out at the top. The great fear had been of setting the thatch on fire. The distant noise was like the roar of that rising fire, turning and burning as it mounted some chimney of the sky.

Deerskin and Hareskin held hands. They were frightened. "Scared," said Rafe to himself. "So am I;" and when they asked him to sit with them, if he liked, he did like, and squeezed between them.

They all listened for the thing coming.

"Wendagoo," said Deerskin. Hareskin said it would eat them all, if it found them.

As they listened the thing rumbled into silence; and after the silence there was a single clap of thunder. A little later something began to fall from the sky. It was not the wet of rain, the dry of hail, or the moist coat of snow. There came down upon them the leaves of trees, the twigs, the cones and fruits, small animals and fish, and now and then a branch large enough to break a skull. A mouse landed on Rafe's shoulder, still well and alive, licked its paws and scuttled away. A hundred yards away water fell down, not as rain but as a splash. A twist of black feathers

84

drifted down, flying without their bird.

There was a swirl in the air, as if it had been flipped over, and then the night's normal slow wind began again.

"Wendagoo," said Hareskin, when the thing had gone, the fall of strange rain was over. She had a great laugh about it, glad to be alive. Wendagoo had always eaten people, until now, she said, going round under the trees, picking mice, fish, squirrels of several kinds, from the ground and from branches, like strange fruit. "Now we eat Wendagoo." She laughed again when she was bitten. Wendagoo the size of a vole was eating her, she thought. Rafe had an uncomfortable sensation about something so small, that could be held in the hand, making a noise so large, shaking the hills. Hareskin let the vole go.

"Wendagoo doesn't like white boys," said Deerskin. And that seemed to explain the matter.

They had days and days more of walking, down the river and along the lake again. Looking across it Rafe saw where they had been before, and that side looked as this side had.

They passed among the great trees again, and through them, climbing mountains, fording streams, wading the flooded bogs of the lowlands. The weather was warmer. There were wet days when they sat in the tent, the women sewing or making traps, teaching Rafe the signs of their language, and the words of it. He learnt them but did not say so, because all they were doing was making him a better slave in the end.

His boots came to pieces. One day he limped along with nails puncturing his foot, and the next the sole and heel fell away entirely. Hareskin made him moccasins from new leather she carried. Not long afterwards Deerskin had to make him leather trousers. When she fitted them to him she pushed and stretched and stuck thorny pins in him just as Mrs Considine would have done, just like any mother, he supposed.

Once, far away, he heard a rifle shot. Another time they thought they saw a sail on the lake. On both occasions they hid for a day. Rafe enjoyed himself. If it was not for the slavery at the end he would have wanted to stay, walking the countryside, doing some small hunting, sleeping under a bush, learning what to eat, where to walk, the things he could see.

One day they all smelt smoke, coming up the lake on the wind. Smoke, Rafe thought, and candles, and another smell he did not care for.

Deerskin and Hareskin thought they were now coming to the end of their journey. Rafe thought that the smell he did not like must be the smell of slaves. He thought he might run away now, and stood alone by the lake for a long time, waiting for one leg to start running for freedom and the other to follow it. But they would not go. He knew what the trouble was: not that he had tried running away and hated it, but that he had grown fond of these two Indian women, because they had been bringing him up to live from the land, and had been kind to him in their own way. He had a thought that when he was a slave he might still see them and be able to sit by their fireside now and then. So his legs only took him back to their fireside now, and then sat him down against it. It was as good as home.

He was glad he had not run away again. Deerskin had been making some sort of garment for several days, and Hareskin had been adding ornaments to it, laces and pieces of glittering stone, blue and white beads, a fur collar. Now the garment was finished.

Instead of putting it on herself Deerskin put it on Rafe. Hareskin took his own coat away and cut the buttons off it. Rafe stood up dressed like an Indian boy, light, warm, and fresh. He carefully said thank you by shaking hands with both ladies, and then they had supper.

Two days later the smell of smoke was strong in the air.

There was the creaking of a Red River cart, two miles away, and later they found its track, with the hoofprints of an ox. Hareskin followed the cart track and picked up a handful of barley grains, one by one, and boiled them for supper. They had not tasted anything breadlike in a long time.

The next day they spent in a little thicket, waiting and getting ready. They were interrupted only by a man passing with a gun and a dog, about a mile away. Rafe knew that before he travelled with the Indian women he would not have noticed a man a mile away. I noticed the dog, he said to himself. The dog did not notice me. The Indian women talked about eating the fat dog of the white man.

The next day they saw a village of wooden houses down the bay. Rafe thought it would be Frenchmen, and he would be a slave there. Then he felt that he had been here before, that he had walked beside this shore and along this headland.

It was here, in the winter, that he and Tawena had come to look at the bear, the day they had got on the ice and been lost, a day in the winter and now summer was coming. The village ahead was no French settlement but his own place, where he had lived, and where he would live again.

He wanted to run ahead, but Deerskin would not let him.

"We will take you in," she said. "That will be safe for us. And you are dressed like an Indian, so be careful."

So they walked to the gateway together, and no one knew Rafe. In the gateway men stood, watching the three Indians they could see. When Rafe came close he found that his own people had a strange strong smell he did not much like. He led the way through, and no one knew him. Deerskin and Hareskin walked behind him now, alarmed at being among the houses near men with guns, men who had been known to shoot Indians. The men with guns watched carefully, Indians had been known to kill men from the villages.

Rafe went straight home. He thought that no one else would be interested in him, only his mother and father. He came to the house where, in the snow, Tawena had tried to catch the crow. The same crow was on the roof. And the same smoke came from the chimney.

Rafe opened the door and went in.

It was like going into a box, a trap. Rooms were something he had forgotten. But here he was in a dark place suddenly.

"And who is it, at all?" said Mrs Considine, who was beside the fire stitching at a stocking.

"It's me, mother," said Rafe, and the words of his own language sounded strange in his ears. He wondered if he had spoken sense, because Mrs Considine only looked at him, drawing the needle out of the sock and stretching her arm out and out until the thread dropped out of its eye. Then the needle tinkled down sparkling into the hearth, the sock went the other way, and Mrs Considine had wrapped Rafe up in her arms. Drops of water fell on his face, and no one said anything for quite a long time. Rafe had no breath to speak with because his mother was squeezing him, and she had no words to say except his name.

Then she let go, and Rafe straightened his tunic.

"And what is it you're wearing?" said Mrs Considine. "How do you think I'll know you dressed like a native? And now tell me what it was all about going off with that Indian girl. If she's outside again I'll lift her off the step for all time, and the pair of you how could you do it to me?"

It was a long time before Rafe could tell his mother about Deerskin and Hareskin. Then she said, "That's a tale; all you've done is start to wander and break your mother's heart and you the only one."

88

Rafe took her outside, because by now she was ready to tell everyone how he had come back.

"No," she said, when Rafe brought her to Deerskin and Hareskin, "I don't have dealings with Indians. That's not the way at all, and it won't do."

"Well, mother," said Rafe, quite loud and clear, "they saved my life, and if you won't help them now then I shall, and go off with them again."

thirteen

"You're very bold now," said Mrs Considine. "And very changed all of a sudden. I'm not sure it's just a very good thing at all."

But she stopped, clamping her arms across her apron, and looked at Hareskin and Deerskin who stood over the road from her. Rafe could tell that they did not see his mother, or the village, in any way he understood, and that their minds were miles away. They had come for something and would go as soon as they had it. The village was a place they did not like, did not approve of, and longed to leave. Their faces were wooden, their eyes watchful. They had been here long enough. Rafe wondered if they were ashamed to be here.

He understood too that he was not going to be sold as a slave. He had misunderstood. All that Hareskin and Deerskin wanted for him was a reward, some return for their trouble or kindness. That was what the bear had told them on the night that Tawena had visited him. That was what they had told him but he had not understood, that night in the forest. They had brought him back to gain a present, not because they liked him. But he was sure that at the end they had liked him.

"They'll want something for you, no doubt," said Mrs Considine. "Well, of course, I'll give them something, yet I don't know what, but what's done now is done soonest."

She saw Mrs Ash from one of the other houses, and called to her that Rafe was back. Mrs Ash, coming running, told others, until there was a crowd gathering.

There were white men and women, Indian women from the tents, Indian children who never go to school, and in the middle, tall and still, their skin clothes drawn close against themselves, were Deerskin and Hareskin. They were uneasy about being surrounded, and so was Rafe. He could hear the story going wrong, and tell that it was turning against his two friends, and that they were to be blamed for things they had not done. It seemed they were not even to be thanked.

"Buying and selling him, that's what," said Mrs Considine. "It would be Christian to hand him to us and say nothing."

"It'd be Christian to help them on their way with a gift," Mrs Ash was saying. "That would be on your side, Mrs Considine. They're pagans, you know, and they haven't a belief worth a pudding-string."

"Will I thank them, and that be enough?" said Mrs Considine. "Taking my boy away and bringing him back so I hardly know him – they'll have stolen his clothes, or where are they?"

"What's a few rags, when all's said and done?" said Mrs Ash. "You have the boy himself, starved and thin. You can send themselves away with your thanks, and that'll do."

"I could send them with less," said Mrs Considine. "If I send them away without complaining of what they did, wouldn't they be lucky and shouldn't that be enough?"

"Or they'll be at it again," said Mrs Ash. "Have we to run them out of the town?" And the whole crowd looked at the Indian women.

Rafe was beginning to shout back at his mother, who was no better than the rest, when the village manager came from his office to find out the truth of the matter. He was the man responsible for seeing that the villagers lived in peace with the Indians, and that the Indians lived in peace with the villagers in spite of having their land stolen from them, or being beaten by villagers who felt it was the right thing to do.

"Now, what is it?" he asked. "It's that runaway boy back, I see." He would always speak like that, making a joke of things so that people were not so intense and angry. "But only the boy knows what happened. So what is it, Rafe?"

Rafe told of going to look at the bear; of the night in the hut on the ice; of landing on the shore of the lake; of how Tawena had stolen his knife and run off, saying she would be killed; how she had come back.

"And then she was killed," he said. It was simple to know the words, but not easy to say them. He felt they were the hardest words he had had to say, because now he told the story of the night in the hut he recalled how Tawena had looked after him, how she had been ready to walk up to the bear herself, to save him, and how he must be wrong about her stealing the knife, though he knew that was what she had done. It was hard to say that she was killed, and when he did say it his throat knotted up and his nose became wet.

"An Indian girl," said Mrs Considine. "I've nothing against them myself, but she was only from the tents yonder."

"Well, she's not here to say a word for herself," said the

manager. "And it sounds as if she helped as much as she could and had a sorry death. Rafe, you've been with these ladies many days, I gather. Tell us how it went on, whether they did you any harm, and why you took so long to come back. If there's anything you ought to tell us tell us at once, so we know exactly how to treat with these ladies."

"Ladies, is it?" said Mrs Considine.

"May you be treated as a lady when you are with them," said the manager. "Now hush, and Rafe will tell us."

"They brought me back," said Rafe. "It was that girl they would kill if they caught her."

"We know nothing of that," said the manager. "Did they treat you well? Did they feed you?"

"Not every day," said Rafe. He did not expect everyone to shout with anger when he said that, but they did, and looked at his friends as if they had been cruel. "When we got food we all had it together. Sometimes there was a lot, sometimes there was nothing."

"That can't be helped, as we all know," said the manager. "Did they treat you well apart from that? Did they give you any cruelty?"

"Of course not," said Rafe. "They are my friends. Now they expect something."

"They deserve it," said the manager. "But we don't know what they want, so can you find out? Somewhere between what they think you're worth, and what we think, will be about right."

Rafe had no difficulty making Deerskin understand. Hareskin was a little more frightened and wanted to be away, but Rafe held the fur of her coat. Deerskin knew what they both wanted, but they did not get it at once.

The village manager sent everyone away but Rafe, his mother, and the two Indian women, because there was too much noise, and some people were out to make trouble.

Indian children were about to begin stealing from villagers' pockets. The Indian women were happier not to be crowded. Also, if anything had been taken by the children the women would probably have got nothing, because every Indian paid for any Indian's misdeeds.

The reward they wanted was one of the village ponies and two lengths of wood.

"Will one be enough, then?" said Mrs Considine, when she heard. "It's what I call a little above themselves themselves is getting."

Rafe's father was sent for during all the gathering and talking. He was glad to see Rafe and gave him a large thump that knocked his breath out of him, a blow much worse than any Hareskin had given. Mr Considine was the village blacksmith, used to beating metal.

"The boy will be worth something," he said. "Would they not rather keep him instead, though? It's a lot of reward for a young ruffian that never brought any good to his parents beyond showing them the true sense of sorrow by his conduct."

"We must show the natives we will treat them fairly," said the manager. "If they have come round the head of the lake they have done a great deal for us, and we must do something for them. Some of it is your duty, blacksmith, and the rest is for the whole village. You and Mrs Considine should put up half the reward, and the Company will see to the rest."

"That makes it reasonable," said Mrs Considine. "It was a big thing else."

"But of course you would have paid," said Mrs Ash, who had gone and come back, liking to make a crowd, and stir up trouble.

"Indeed," said Mrs Considine, giving Rafe a hug he did not want. He was more used to the quiet and restrained ways of Deerskin and Hareskin.

"Then there'll be a village pony in the stable," said the manager. "We'd best go there next."

The Indian women were not given a choice of ponies. The manager brought one out and that was it. It was sound, healthy, well-fed, and for Deerskin and Hareskin it was Yes or No.

"Take or leave," said Mr Considine, lifting the pony's foot and looking at it. There was work for him on the pony, which had to have its shoes removed to make it suitable for work in the wilderness. There were no smiths beyond the village.

"And two poles," said Rafe.

"Yes, yes," said the manager, knowing exactly what were wanted and fetching them.

Deerskin attached them to the harness so that they trailed from the pony's shoulders and on the ground behind. She rode the pony, Hareskin rode the poles. It was called a travoy. They were given a paring knife and a rasp, to keep the pony's hoofs in order.

"I think they want one more thing," said Rafe, sending his mother off for a whole bag of meal, because he had longed for bread on the journey, and the Indian women had been delighted when they found a few grains of barley. "And I'll buy them a coil of tobacco," he said. "One day I'll pay for it." He put the coil beside the meal, on the travoy.

The Indian women were ready to go. Hands were shaken all round, even by Mrs Considine. "I never saw that before," said the manager. "Not handshaking. It's a trick they had from Rafe. They'll be learning to knock on doors next."

Rafe knew they had held his hands, not shaken them. He could not say anything to them in case he began to cry.

That was that. It was over. Deerskin and Hareskin rode off. Rafe would have run with them a mile or two, to see them on their way, but Mrs Considine held his arm. Now that she had him again she would keep him, she declared. Of the Indian women she said, "They think we can't tell from their faces they're pleased. But we can: they're like children, and that's the top and bottom of the matter with Indians."

Rafe went away by himself for a time, "I will not cry, even to myself," he said. But a sneeze, or something, ran down his cheek and he wiped it away.

Later in the day, when the other boys were in school still, Rafe was doing nothing in the street, full of the strange food of home, as if nothing had happened in the past months except a change in the clothes he was wearing, and a change too in the way he looked at things, in what he heard, in the smells he picked up. But otherwise some queer holiday had come and gone and left him as he was.

All at once, seeing one of the tent Indian girls in the street, he thought about Tawena. He had not thought of her for a long time, and there had been nothing he could do if he had. But still he felt guilty. He knew he would think of her again, and he hoped he could forgive her for taking his knife. She would stay in his mind, a fat-filled face, leading him into danger; and he would always remember, he knew, how she stole his knife, how it must lie in the forest now, lost, buried, never to be seen again. I am sorry for that, he thought. I am sorry she was killed.

He thought that Tawena must have pitied the way he could not follow in her tracks when they went to look at the bear. After all, it had taken a great deal of effort later to stop Hareskin banging his back.

He thought how Tawena must have been full of scorn at his conduct in the hut as he jumped about like a fool; he blushed at the memory of fainting when he saw the bear in the doorway. He had not thought how they were to stay alive; but Tawena had known what to do.

He saw, as if it was happening again, that Tawena had despised him when they reached the shore again; he had gone about laughing like an idiot, tearing up lumps of damp smoky stuff for the fire. "She will have hated me," he thought. "But she did her best to save me, and she did."

But if she had lived, how would it have been?

fourteen

After Rafe and Tawena had come on to dry land again, on to the firm ground, after the ice had brought them over the waves of the lake, after the hut had fallen all round them, Tawena was careless. But not careless enough to die.

It was easy to be careless. She had stood all night by the hot stove; she had known what happened when a brown bear put claws and teeth into a child, because she had seen it happen to a boy in camp. And she knew that whatever she did now, however she tried to get back to her own people in the village the far side of the lake, it would be very difficult with a wild boy like Rafe, who knew nothing about staying alive in the real world outside a house.

She looked at him now. He had no idea what to do, where to go, how to do it if he had known. He was tramping about on the lake shore, making noises, kicking snow and stone, waiting for things to come right for him.

"The white people do not think," said Tawena to herself. "Their faces are pale and their hearts do not work. He is, moreover, dancing like a bear." She looked round for the bear for herself. That creature had gone on down the shore of the lake. Now they were all on dry land it went away as soon as it could.

Tawena's instincts were working. She saw and heard many more things than Rafe did, looking and listening, watching and being aware, sniffing and smelling, feeling the wind and weather, searching the sky.

She saw and heard the hut collapsing. "Rayaf," she said to herself, "do not make more noise than the things we are listening for," but Rafe was laughing as the hut fell down and was torn apart, when he should have been helping to plan, helping for what was to come, not looking at what was gone.

"This ground, this snow, is broken by Rayaf's feet," Tawena told herself. "I shall kick it more and find a fire stone, and then with Rayaf's knife make a fire."

She found a fire stone and asked Rafe for his knife. He did not understand what Tawena said, to begin with, and when he did understand he did not want to let her have the knife.

"Rayaf does not know that if we are together everything is for both of us," Tawena thought, but she could not say it, because Rafe would not know her words. "What shall we do," she wondered, "when I need the knife again to save our lives, and Rayaf will not let me have it? But then," she told herself, "I did not bring with me anything but my bare hands and what I know, and best of all, a little tinder."

When she began to make sparks into the tinder Rafe shouted at her.

"He is worse than a bear," she thought. "In fact a bear would have more sense than to make such noise. A bear is a wise creature and, if it knew how, it too would make fire. But that is a different sense."

Rafe seemed to understand slowly what she was doing. He began to look for fuel to burn, bringing out roots like stones, branches like rock, damp blocks of old grass. He stopped when she looked at him. It was no use talking to him in her own language, and she did not know enough of his to explain. "And how could I explain," she thought, "to people who know nothing? And I have no breath now I am blowing on the fire to make it burn." She let the fire grow in a cradle of dry twigs she had gathered so easily and quickly, without scraping the ground, without tearing the world open, without leaving a trace.

"Bear," she said to Rafe. "Ever mad bear."

She blew at the fire again, and used one or two pieces from what Rafe had brought.

"If I am to get him home I must not make him angry," she thought. "It will need both of us if we are to stay alive, because I am not sure I can stay alive by myself, and I know he cannot. We should now walk up the lake and across the river that comes into it, and down the other side, and somewhere is his village, up in the wind." She looked at the smoke from the fire, seeing how it blew off the water, taking the smoke across the land, through the trees.

She realised she did not know what was among those trees.

"Rayaf," she said, to give him something to do, and because it might be useful, and because there might not be another chance for doing it, "get ever bit," and she pointed to the hut, where it lay collapsed in the water, partly rooted in ice, partly floating, partly shipwrecked on the rocks.

While Rafe looked doubtfully at the wood, which was still joined in large sections, Tawena heard something she did not want to hear.

She heard voices. She heard words she understood.

Quietly, not far away, two Indian women, of her own kind, were conversing as they walked in the forest.

Bears were one thing. It is possible to go away from a bear. It is possible to frighten a bear away. A bear will forget you.

A bear does not want you dead; it does not want to kill you, though it will if it is hungry, or angry, and you are in its way.

But Tawena knew why she and her own family lived with the white men in the village, not with their own group in the swamps, prairies, and forests. They had dropped out of the tribe, because the rules were too hard for them to obey. The rule they had broken was to let Tawena live. There were too many girls in the tribe, and baby girls were not to live. Tawena had lived. Her mother had taken her to the white man's village. Because of that she was not marked with the cheek-cuts of those allowed to live, so Indian women, and men too, would kill her if she was found in the wilderness – though they dared not do so in the village.

Here, by the lake, there would be a quick blow with a knife of stone, and Tawena would not come home. Rafe, very likely, would not do so either. He would live, but only as a slave or servant among the Indians, being exchanged, perhaps, for some small useful thing.

"Rayaf," said Tawena, still listening, thinking that he would not fetch very much when he was sold because he was not good at useful tasks.

Rafe looked at her. He had heard nothing at all. It was as if he was old and deaf, like some dog fit only for stew, Tawena thought. She wanted him to make no noise, to put the fire out, to ask Maneto to send the smoke where it would not be smelt or tasted by the women. Tawena knew the smoke would be on the trees for days, and on the snow for weeks, perhaps, where any Indian could feel it with their fingers, never mind with tongue or nose.

Rafe made a noise. He said, "Hey," which meant he was about to speak.

"That is the way of the white people," Tawena thought. "First they make a loud noise with no meaning, and then they say something that does not need to be said. Words are like beads to them; they wear them all over themselves."

Before Rafe managed to speak Tawena heard the Indian women taste the smoke and say the word for it. She heard nothing from them after that, and knew they would be coming to the fire. She told Rafe that they were coming, that she had never been there, that he would live with them, and must say nothing about her. She slipped away along the edge of the lake, through and among the bushes growing there, her feet silent under water-washed stone, her head carefully not shaking snow from overhanging branches.

From among rocks she watched.

Rafe followed her track for a little way and then could not see it at all. That meant nothing. It was likely that the Indian women could follow.

"If they follow," said Tawena to herself, "I shall not run away any further. I shall walk to them and give them Rayaf's knife, and with it they shall kill me. First I will tell them to take Rayaf back to his own village and perhaps tell my people to sing to Maneto for me. It is all in the hands of Maneto now."

She saw Rafe do nothing useful. He went back to the fire and put wet stuff on it so that it smoked. "Even a white man could come to that fire now," thought Tawena.

The Indian women came. There were two of them, a mother and a daughter. They both had the cheek-cuts of those allowed to live. To Tawena they looked like two widows ranging free on a spring walkabout, trapping animals for skins, or gathering herbs.

They came up to Rafe as he knelt over the fire. The mother stood over him. Tawena could not understand how Rafe did not know, how he could not have heard. But he did not know. When he did look up his action was pathetic and ridiculous. He behaved like some simple-minded animal, smiling at the Indian woman, thinking he had been rescued, saved, set on his way home.

The smile soon went away. The Indian woman looked at him, searching his face for sense, not at all friendly like the white people. Rafe turned to run away, but the daughter was behind him, to hold him by the hair and by an ear.

He squealed. He squalled. "And that is how it would be," said Tawena to herself, "if you are caught. But what next, Rayaf?" She watched. "If the knife comes out," she thought, "I shall run forward and tell them he is worth much good reward. And when he is at the village he will tell my people how the knife came on me. That is the way it will be."

The Indian mother trampled out the fire, looked at the hut on the water, found nothing of use in it, and came back to help the daughter tie Rafe's thumbs together behind his back.

Tawena stayed where she was. Rafe was to be kept alive, she saw. He was marched off, the mother in front, the daughter behind him, into the trees and away from the lake shore.

Tawena sat for a long time on a rock, listening, waiting, thinking. The cold wind that had broken and melted the ice blew round her, but she did not shiver. The emptiness of her stomach was painful but she took no notice.

She thought instead. At last she took the knife, Rafe's knife, and examined if carefully.

She had used the back of the blade to strike sparks with.

Now she looked at the edge. It was a good knife, made by the village's blacksmith, one of his best in fact, because he was Rafe's father. Rafe had not kept the blade at all well. A white boy did not need a knife to stay alive with. He had it for a toy, and a wooden one would do almost as well as a steel one. It had a blunt edge, like the white boy himself, no sharpness.

Tawena stood up, stiff with cold, to search for the right rock.

With it, by the darkening light of the northern afternoon, she set an edge on the blade, an edge that would slice the length of a hair. As darkness began to gather far over the water she used the new edge, shaping a strip of bark to make a sheath for the blade.

She followed the track Rafe had made as he was led away, a thing easy to do.

"Rayaf going like bear still," she said, seeing one clumsy mark after another. All round her the trees grew taller as the forest closed on her. She knew how to belong to it, that it was a place where she could live, perhaps.

"Rayaf," she thought, "will like none of it at all. I shall save him. Now that there are three of us to look after him I think he will be taken to the village, and if he is I shall be too. But only I shall know that; they will never see me." She felt the edge of the knife blade, so sharp, and was frightened, for a time, of what she had to do with it that same night, to herself.

fifteen

"A day ago," Tawena reminded herself, "a day ago and we went to look at a bear on the headland, asleep, just waking after the winter." She and her mother had found the bear during the winter, hearing it move in its sleepy underground place, that no white man knew about, although the place could be seen from the village. Tawena had gone to tease the bear, to startle Rafe. She had set out on an idle, harmless errand of mischief.

One day ago, and a whole wide lake away, and now the bear was carried away, Tawena was carried away, and was cold in a far distant forest, where the tree tops cut black into the blue sky; and there was nothing to eat.

Tawena told herself not to think of food. She followed the track of Rafe, where he had walked with one woman in front and the other behind. Their prints were not to be seen; no trace was left of where they had been; but where Rafe had rambled there was a track like a landslide. Tawena felt she could follow it in the dark.

She hoped she was right in her guess and that the two women were out alone, trapping.

"I can save Rayaf if they are alone," she said, though not out loud. "If they are from a big party, a camp or hunting group, I can do nothing. Shall I get back to my people, if that is so?"

That was something she thought about as she went through the trees. Nothing moved except herself. All animals had been driven into hiding by Rafe's noisy walking.

Tawena walked on, alone, no sounds anywhere, wondering whether she was awake. She thought, "If there are men and women in a camp perhaps I shall use the knife to make cheek-cuts, which will take many weeks to heal and look old, and see whether the people accept me. If not, they will kill me; moreover, I shall be dead long before that, of cold. Dogs, boys, men, or worse, women, will find me close by, and that will be my journey."

Most of all she knew it would be wrong to pretend to be something she was not. If her father, if her mother, had wanted they could have made cheek-cuts below her eyes and a little to one side; but that would have been worse than staying alive when you were meant not to live.

Tawena had been walking along nearly asleep. She heard Rafe somewhere ahead, loud enough to have been heard long before by anyone fully awake.

She stopped walking. Rafe was crying, sobbing. He was frightened, and he was in pain: he was alone, with his thumbs tied behind his back.

The Indian women were not with him. Tawena saw the skin tent, smelt the small fire and lay flat, because the women were out hunting, noiselessly, invisibly, where they might catch Tawena herself. They would not think twice, they would not think once, about putting a knife in her neck. They would not bury her, they would not even take her scalp. They would think she was dead already, with no cheek-cuts; not allowed to live is as good as dead.

The women came back to the tent. There were two of them only, and no more. Tawena was sure now that they were working alone.

"It is three of us, to keep him," she said. "Surely I can manage it." She thought with dread of what had to be done, what she had to do to herself, of how she must be right in everything.

The women cooked something over the fire. They had found a rotten tree and dug in the soft wood for wood-grubs, long and black, crisp and fatty when roasted. They had a bag of them, spluttering and stiffening over the flames. Tawena could smell the musky smell. Her mouth filled with water; deep inside her stomach asked for help.

Rafe was given wood-grubs to eat, on a plate of bark. His hands were still tied behind him, so he ate with his mouth like a dog.

"Bear," said Tawena to herself.

She loved Bear, real Bear, because Bear was the animal of her people. She loved him for his strength and pride, for his greed and anger, for his ferocity and his way of doing all he wanted. But she, and all her people, would laugh at him too, for the way he walked (not caring about his track), for the way he stood up on two legs (Bear taught man how to do that), for the way he would eat (not minding how sticky his jaws got). Now Rafe was eating like Bear.

Overhead the last sunlight climbed into the tops of the trees and then into the clouds only. Tawena had a final look at the little camp, where the women were now using the last of the daylight to make traps and nets, forming the wood in the fire. She curled up where she was and thought of the difficult and painful things she had to do in the dark, without trying them first, without any rehearsal at all: there was only one time to get them right.

A day ago, a night ago, she had been safe in a hut with a stove beside her, with a bear outside. She loved Bear, like all her people, but would he love her without cheek-cuts?

Tawena talked to Maneto for a time, and Maneto sent her sleep.

When she woke she lay still with her eyes closed. She hoped it would now be morning, too late to do what she planned. But when her eyes were open she saw the light of all the stars, each light small enough to come down between the leaves and branches, each small enough to sit on the frosts on the tree bark, to dance on the knife blade when she unsheathed it. It was still night.

Cautiously she crawled from where she slept. Slowly she stood up. She opened her mouth and breathed with an open throat, so that she could not hear herself. She walked towards the camp.

As she went she looked ahead at the things she had to do, going through them in her mind. All of them could go wrong; or all of them could go right and she could still be dead. She did not want to be dead, because she wanted to know whether things happened right.

She walked on, to do the first thing.

She came very close to the camp. In the back of the tent, which was only a wall of skin with the top draped over a little, the two women slept. To one side Rafe, she saw, had a fold of skin over him. There was frost on his hair, and starlight showed his face.

She came close to him, crawling now, alongside him, the whole length of him, then on top of him, holding him down. He woke, and became very stiff and frightened. He would have called out, but Tawena had her hand on his mouth, on his nose, so that he could not breathe or cry out.

"Rayaf," she said, a whisper in her throat so that only Rafe could hear, "Rayaf," and she said it again and again until he knew what it was, who it was, that had taken hold of him, and he relaxed, ready to be rescued.

When he was ready Tawena told him, in the few words of English that she knew, what she intended to do. She could not tell him exactly, because that was too difficult for her. She said it as nearly as she could.

"Bear come," she said, "Bear will tell Indian womans to take you home. Indian womans will understand. He will take you home. Indian woman he understand what bear say, take Rayaf home, Rayaf give him present, blanket, beans." And she told him the same message as many times as she could. She at last lifted her hand from his mouth, putting it back at once when it seemed that he would speak. But he understood that he had to remain quiet, and lay still and silent, like part of the ground.

Tawena went away from him. Rafe's eyes were looking at hers. She turned her back and walked into the trees, behind the tent.

This was where she had to do the next thing.She chose a place among the undergrowing bushes. She chose it because small branches grew close round about, and because the ground was a little softer under their shelter. When she had looked she came away, leaving no mark as she came and went. Then, working by the light of the stars, she walked like a white boy, but silently, into the middle of the undergrowth, and came out again, smoothing each footprint so that it looked like the mark of a boot.

Watching, listening, in case the women woke, she next made the great track of a brown bear, as if it were walking to the same place. She went on beyond with the same track, and came back again, leaving no mark. Now anyone looking would see how a white boy had come here, a bear had come after him, and only a bear had gone away.

"Maneto listen to me," said Tawena to herself, to Maneto. She started the next thing she had to do. She began a great noise. She ran about, stamping her foot into the frosty ground. She tore off a strip of the brown village dress she wore. She shrieked in fear, she screamed. She growled like a bear. She shook and broke branches, throwing herself down amongst them and against them to make them snap and whip. She was acting out a child being caught by a bear, and eaten.

The worst part of that came at the end. Tawena had meant to pretend to die with a whimper, gradually, but the knife was part of what she had to do, because there must be blood. When she lifted the bright blade and cut herself deep the length of her fore-arm, the sudden burning pain, the hot and cold of the blade and the blood, made her scream the loudest scream. And that was all from her, because she was now meant to be dead. She had to be dead. Rafe had to think she was dead.

So there was blood. The stars went out, and darkness came. Tawena felt she would fall over in faintness. But she had to go on with what she was doing, because this part was not finished and there was more to come. She forced herself not to go into the blackness, not to fall. She had to grind her own bones in the mouth of the bear. She did it with her own teeth and her own throat. Then the bear had to be made to walk away, along the path prepared for it.

Tawena thought she had perhaps truly killed herself with the knife, that she would die of that wound very soon. When she had stopped being the bear she tore off more dress and wrapped it round the arm.

While she could still smell blood, she made her way back to the women's camp, and became a bear again, snuffling and sniffing, and with the handle of the knife making the noise of bear's claws on roots and fallen wood.

She did more than that. She spoke. She said words. She said them as a bear would say them, like a bear that was more than real, like a bear that was part of Maneto, or the messenger of the spirits of the forest.

She spoke deep and loud, like a shout. She spoke in her own language. The women would hear the bear speaking in that language, the same as their own, and would understand. So the bear spoke, deep and horrible.

"Take the white boy," it said, "take him back to his people beyond the lake. There was another child but I have eaten him. Take this one back, and you will be given wheat and tobacco. This is what the bear says."

"Do not come nearer," said the mother. "We smell the blood on you. We shall do as you say."

"Many days," said the other woman. "Many days along the lake and down the far side."

"The bear will watch you," said Tawena. Then that was enough for her to say, and she could only grunt a little, and slowly go away into the forest, chilled, sick, ill, the pain of the steel cut down her arm, the knife cold in her other hand. She could not have walked quietly if she had wanted.

"I am about to die," she said, and lay under a rock, ready to do so, if Maneto wished it.

sixteen

Left to itself the wilderness is clean. Tawena's arm had a deep but simple cut. When the sun came out it shone on her and warmed her; she was hidden from the wind; as she lay thirsting water dripped from a crust of ice on a ledge above her, and she could catch it in her hand.

She washed her mouth. She washed her arm. The cut grew a long dark raised line, and there was a long gentle ache there too.

By the time the sun had risen to its fullest height and then begun to fall again, Tawena had rested. She was now only thirsty, thirstier than the drops of water could keep up with, with a clogged and sticky taste in her mouth.

She got up from where she lay and wrapped her blanket round her. She was sure she left some of her warmth behind her in the ground. She began to walk, with a dizziness making her wonder whether she could stay upright. The trees seemed to sway from side to side, the forest floor lifted and fell.

But before long, by walking, she made herself stronger, made her feet steady, made her head balance better.

She followed her own bear-like tracks towards the camp where the women had Rafe. Now that she was fully awake, and walking, she was anxious about him. She could not tell whether what the bear said had made the Indian women do what she wanted. Had they understood? Had they believed? Had they wanted to do it even if they understood and believed?

There was a smell of dead fire among the trees, hanging in the air as it would for many hours, hanging on the needles of the fir trees if you touched and tasted them, as it would for many days.

The camp had gone. The tent was taken away, the fire stamped out. There was warmth in the place, and Tawena, when she had walked warily to the hearth, looking and listening in case there was a trap, put her hands on warm turf, under the turf, in the hidden ashes, hoping for a spark to blow on, some fire ready to raise.

"For," she said to herself, "I dare not light a fresh fire in another place in case they are near and smell it and know I made it: I can only use their flame and listen while I do so, and the worst that can happen is that one of them will come back and stamp the fire out, thinking they left it burning."

Today there was no spark, no fire could be lifted from the grey ash, the black charcoal.

Tawena rested longer than she meant. She was weaker than she thought. She looked for something to eat, but there was nothing. Then a pine cone fell close by, and in its leathery scales, its wooden feathers, were hidden the white pine nuts. She picked them out one by one, tearing the cone apart. That was her meal for this day and the day before.

She curled up where she was, in no shelter at all, to sleep

for a time. With the sun only its own width down the sky she woke up, no longer weak but still thirsty.

She looked at her own tracks, where the bear had walked to the camp; where it had fought and eaten her among the bushes.

In the soft sheltered snow under the trees, where it fell gently and had not been blown, or melted and refrozen, the bear prints looked huge, as bear prints are, but not very distinct, which was how they would be in that whiteness. Tawena saw how the Indian women had come up to look at the prints, making their own delicate marks, and trampled over them were Rayaf's impressions, not at all like a bear, but more like a bear than like an Indian boy.

She looked at her own blood on the snow. Something had been eating it. She remembered that she was alone in the wilderness, and there were things that would eat lonely people. Not every creature was known about, for certain.

The track of the women and Rayaf was easy to follow. "Even a white man would have seen it," Tawena thought. "Rayaf has kicked it up so much that I could follow in the dark by feeling the ground."

The women had not gone far. Long before night came on Tawena found the new place, behind a natural hedge of bushes. Before she found it she had seen and heard one of the Indian women, the mother, who had stalked and caught a deer, bringing it down with an arrow. Tawena watched her take the arrow out, clean the stone point, and hide it away. The woman went on looking for other things to catch.

Tawena went on following the track in a zig-zag, crossing it from side to side, so that her own prints would not be on it very often.

Rafe stood in that night's camp, alone. Tawena was glad to see him alive, with his arms no longer tied. He looked

114

miserable, tired, unhappy, and he was too easy to see.

"He has no idea of being out of sight," thought Tawena. She called to him, but thought it best to call like a bear. She was good at bear noises, because Bear was the animal of her people.

"Rayaf looks round and is frightened," she said.

Rafe sat down, not at all hidden. He fell over, but that was his way of going to sleep. Tawena listened. No Indian women could be heard. She went to the camp where Rafe was lying. She crossed snowy ground to him and looked.

"He is too much a white man to be woken," she told herself. "He will cry out; and I am not strong enough to hold him as I held him last night. But he is not hurt; he is well. I think the women are taking him to his own tribe, and therefore I can follow; in this way there is safety for both of us."

She came out of the camp again backwards, drawing where it would show the track of a bear behind her. She hid herself away in the forest to watch the women come back at dusk. They became angry with Rafe. He had been meant to light a fire, but had not done so.

"There is little he knows," said Tawena, as she saw him pushed over. She heard them scold him. She saw the flames rising, and heard the wood crack. She smelt the meat roasting, and pine nuts rattled in her stomach. She drank water that ran under the ice, all that there was. She slept under her shawl. That and her leggings kept the cold away.

In the morning she was lucky. The Indian women and Rafe got up when there was light and left the camp, taking the tent, making their day's journey. The fire was kicked down, but Tawena came to it before it was cold, before it was out, and put it together warmer, to glow without flame, without smoke. Now far away she found many pieces of deer, a whole mouse, and a bundle of roots, stuff that would not be carried away in a well-stocked forest. From it all she made herself a full and hot meal.

Her arm was stiff and tender and not very useful, but the only pain was the pain of healing.

Then she followed the women closely, so closely that once she arrived at their path ahead of them and had to wait until they went past. At one part of the journey there was a strange noise.

"Rayaf is singing with his lips, a white man noise," Tawena said to a small bird. "Look." She and the bird looked and saw how the daughter thumped his back and the mother twisted his face for him, and the noise stopped. "And Rayaf is cross," said Tawena. The Indian women were cross too.

Later they halted for the night. The women left to hunt. Tawena watched Rafe, who was left behind and did not know what to do, or perhaps how to do it. "They will return in a little while. If they become too angry they will forget what they are doing with Rayaf," thought Tawena. "Rayaf does not know this very well. He is going to sleep again and has made no fire, and that is very foolish. White men are like this. No doubt they think of something, but what it is they do not know. They talk so much all the wisdom runs out of their mouths. But *I* know there should be a fire, and if there is not there will be something worse for him."

While Rafe slept Tawena made fire out in the forest, carried the smouldering tinder to where he lay, and put a small fire in the place where fire had been before.

"So the women know all this land," she said. "Rayaf will do well. I shall do well." She left Rafe asleep and went back among the trees.

In a little while Rafe whistled again. "He has forgotten so soon," said Tawena. "They do not use their hearts, white men."

She could not tell him to be quiet. When the Indian women came back the daughter thumped him, and the mother twisted his face.

The bird with blue wings, that Tawena had spoken to before, flew close and gave a whistle of its own. This time the mother hit Rafe, and the daughter pulled his face.

"Well now, bird," said Tawena, "be glad you are not a white man's child."

The next day Tawena saw Rafe make fire for himself, without being asked, without anger being shown him. This day they had all walked further, and Rafe did not fall asleep.

They were in a thin part of the forest. There was not much to eat in the camp that night, and nothing outside it. The whistling bird pecked anxiously under leaves. In the morning there was nothing edible in the camp, and the fire had dropped to cold ash. Tawena walked hungry that day.

There were days like that. There were days when she followed close by, able to hear what was said at the camp. There were days when she stayed where she was, knowing she could easily follow the track, days when she hunted for her own food, when she thought the women were far enough ahead for her to dare to make her own fire.

Day by day Rafe's track became less of a plough-mark, was more like an Indian's track. But it was still so easy to follow that Tawena had no difficulty. Slowly he grew better at living in the forest. He once caught in his own hands a striped squirrel, and brought it to the mother Indian.

"Rayaf does not know that we do not eat that," said Tawena, to that same bird. The women could not explain very well to Rafe that they could not eat the squirrel. They left it by the track, and walked on.

"The white boy does not understand what they said or why they said it," said Tawena.

She picked up the little animal and roasted it, though she knew it was a creature that may not be eaten.

That night, like an answer to doing some wrong thing, a grey shape came silently to her in the night and sniffed at her.

She woke, and there was wolf gazing into her eyes, and more of his tribe beside him, all looking at her.

"Wolf does not eat Indian," Tawena thought. But she remembered that Indian did not eat striped squirrel, and she had done that. So what might wolf do?

seventeen

Wolf sniffed at Tawena. She wondered whether wolf's mouth was wetting with wanting to eat her. One wolf, then another – the first one stepping aside, licking his jaws as if he had eaten – sniffed at her face, her breath.

Tawena was curled up on the ground under a snowy bush. Above her the branches were joined together with a shining thin webby dome, where warmth from her had melted the snow and ice had formed. Moonlight came down through the trees, hanging in the cloudy air and making more stars and more in the frost on the bush.

Tawena looked at that. She looked at wolf, one wolf and then another. By the time the seventh wolf came along she was so much awake that she had to move, because the ground was hard.

She sat up propped on one arm. The movement startled the wolves, and they retreated half a dozen wolf paces, still with their faces towards her. They were cautious but not afraid.

They came forward again, all together, all looking and breathing the air round her. She fell down on her side once more, but not on purpose. She was holding herself up with the cut arm, but it was not strong enough, and let her go. The wolves backed off again. Three of them turned away, wanting to be somewhere else, and four of them only put their faces forward, mouths open.

The three that wanted to be away danced with impatience, but they were the young ones; the elders still looked at Tawena and thought about her.

Tawena got up slowly. She was on all fours, like a wolf. She knelt up on her knees, and they raised their heads to look in her eyes. She raised herself further, on one knee, and then stood up.

The wolves stood in a circle round her when she walked into open ground. One by one they sniffed at the clean busy scent of the healing wound on her arm. To Tawena in the moonlight it was a small line on her skin, something she felt no more. To them it was a sign of her taste. Tonight they did not want that; tonight they had paused to remind themselves of mankind, but they had other things in their minds.

In a circle round her they milled about, and began to run, a little way off, and back again, the younger ones leading. The four older ones took longer to go, ran more steadily when they did, as if they expected a long night, a long run.

The greatest of them, the eldest, the leader, looked at her and moved off at last. Before he had gone his own length he stopped in mid stride and looked at her, and ran the same length again, and looked once more.

"Tawena will follow," said Tawena. Whether they meant it or not, whether they wanted her or not, she ran with them, through wolf-high tracks in the forest, in and out of the moonlit mist, the hollow shadows; through long glades like roads, where the trees seemed to stand back on either side; down gentle valleys where a half-frozen stream lay nearly still in a smooth natural meadow; down the twisting ravines running out of the hills, and into the great white plains, where the mist was tangled with nothing and lay in drifts like snow without substance, on the ground, above it, or as clouds overhead.

In the long silences of the journey the trail of wolves never left her, some in front, some behind, usually one beside her, their breath more visible than themselves, their eyes glowing when they looked back to her, their paws whispering on the snow.

In the bitter winter of the open country, where spring had hardly come by night, where no cover of trees held the harsh sky from the ground, like a blanket, there was frozen water on lake and marsh.

Through this marsh, trailing northwards on the edge of winter, went the caribou, their long herds following tracks they knew, that wolf knew, that some Indians might have seen, but no white man would ever learn.

To a place where the way was narrow between hills steamy with cold the wolves came, and the caribou were there too. At the entrance to the narrow place, where frozen lake ran into solid river, the great herd crowded on itself, the way only a few beasts wide. The caribou did not understand about waiting, standing back, giving room. At this place the wolves could come up on creatures not expecting them, and take a slow one, an old one, one that did not watch.

Silently the wolves came. Tawena wondered at that. Why so silent, why no calling, no howling, no wolf speech?

The younger wolves had seen and smelt the caribou. But it was the leader who would direct the attack, who would say which caribou to take. The younger ones wanted to howl, to call, to work themselves to the point of action.

But when they were about to make a noise the eldest wolf seized their throats, to make them understand that no noise must be made. He led them now, making them lurk in any cover there was, in long grass, among rocks, flat on their bellies. One by one the young ones crawled to him to lick the corner of his mouth, because he was their leader, because he was their father or the father of the group, because they expected food from him.

There were other wolves hunting there that night. They sang, they howled, they told the world that this was their hunting, that only they could be in this place, in the middle of their own land.

"We say that," Tawena thought. "We say we are on the land that feeds us; and we go away and come back and the land is waiting for us. The white man says the same, but he never goes away. He thinks the land is his; he does not think he belongs to the land."

She now understood the silence: this was not the territory of the small pack she was with. They were intruders; she was intruding with them. From her own pack she was in no danger; from the others she might be.

She unsheathed the knife. Its blade flashed harder than ice in the moonlight. On the frozen lake a wolf's eye caught the gleam, and all his pack looked.

Tawena's leader now rose and ran forward, a wild scream of daring and defiance coming from him, and more screams from the rest of the pack. Now was their time, or it would have gone; now they must kill, eat and leave, as a wolf does.

There were others hunting here tonight, more of their own kind defending their rightful place. Yet Tawena's own wolves must be from the same pack in the end, because they knew the place, the night to come; and they knew they were intruders, thieves in the night.

There was plenty for all, if they would share. Tawena

ran forward with them, adding her own howl to those of all the wolves.

Her feet, the paws of the wolves, the hooves of the caribou, threw up a fine prickly mist of ice. In this cloud she could not see certainly what happened, but there were wolves fighting wolves, and wolves tearing down one old animal too slow or too alarmed to know where to run. Wolves had surrounded caribou, and now caribou surrounded wolves. But one caribou was down, a leg crippled by a bitten sinew.

Tawena came forward then with the knife, keener than a tooth, and longer, and the caribou sank to the ice, all its legs spread, as if it were only asleep. As life left it the knife came out, black in the moonlight.

Tawena's own wolves then began to eat. She stood on the shoulder of the fallen beast, and it shook under her as each wolf ate as much as it could. They would carry it away in their stomachs, each with half his own weight, and back in the forest disgorge it and chew it in peace.

Tawena could not do that. She could carry meat, however. With the knife and one hand she cut a thick steak, still warm. With the other she hit at wolves she knew were not her own. They did not like to approach her, because she was mankind. She circled round the group, driving off the enemy.

All at once her own wolves left their eating, had a sharp skirmish with the others, and ran back the way they had come. Even by moonlight Tawena saw how they were swollen with what they had devoured.

They followed their own track back the way they had come, up, up, all the way, towards the forest, through the narrow places, where moonlight was now giving place to daylight.

"Sagastao," said Tawena to herself. "The sun rises."

Ahead the sun rose over the forest. When they saw it,

before they came among the thick trees, the wolves stopped, gambolled once more round Tawena, and struck off in a different direction, to the south, their bodies swaying under the load they had eaten. They had said goodbye, and Tawena knew she must not follow any further.

She went on into the rising sun, licking at the huge piece of meat she carried, weary but satisfied.

In full daylight she cleaned the knife, then made fire, and on the fire roasted the meat. She ate as much of it as she could, hiding the rest under some stones for the time being.

After that, with the day beautiful among the branches, she walked about and sang a song to Maneto, for showing her the land she loved, for giving her food, and for fire.

She knew she would have a long sleep. The meat inside her was calling her to rest. She built a small sleeping house, and did the housekeeping of putting leaves and pine branches in it. When the day part of the forest life was beginning, as the air warmed itself, she crawled into the sleeping house, pulled branches round her, and slept.

She woke at night, counted the stars so that she knew where she was, and slept again.

Next time she woke was daylight. Snow melted from tree tops, and she drank that. She ate the other half of the meat, and slept again, because night was coming on.

She woke in daylight once more, a darkened daylight with spring snow falling and filtering down to the ground. All round her there was not a mark, and the gentle powder came silently down, covering the forest floor, covering her sleeping house, keeping her warm.

Inside her she had meat still, so she did not feel hunger. "Maneto has sent snow," she thought, and slept again, through a day and a night, and woke the next day, ready to move again, to hunt again.

"I cannot sleep like Bear all a winter," she said, crawling out into fresh snow and looking about.

Then, seeing the whiteness all round, unmarked, with no tracks, no traces, she remembered that she had never known where she was, only that she had been following a track, that she was a long way from that track, and that it would be covered and invisible by now.

Rafe might get home; but Tawena herself could not follow him there. For herself it was important, though more important still was giving back the knife.

There was no way of knowing where to go; no sun shone through thick cloud, and no mark lay on the ground.

"I have slept longer than a winter," she said. "I have slept until I am dead. That is all."

eighteen

"If I am dead," Tawena thought, "then it is because Maneto has called me. Moreover, it is likely that I died even before I ran with the wolves, and that such hunting is what another life is for."

But in another life you hope to meet those that have gone before, and here there was no one, and nothing moved but the little fall of snow, gentle, peaceful, silent, deadly.

"I have brought the knife," she said. "Maneto, I have brought the knife. But there is nothing I can do with it, and my hunger has come back."

There was silence. Maneto did not speak. But Maneto's silence is as important as his speech, though it is harder to know what he means.

All at once he spoke, Tawena thought. A tree behind her was too full of snow, and the load of one branch slid off, plunging to the ground through other branches, pushing snow off the branches below, shaking the whole tree once as the great mass fell, and then shaking it again as each branch sprang up. All the snow, it seemed, fell from that one tree.

It was a red hemlock. The needles were green at the tips, but coming from the stalks they were red. The tree stood red, the one thing coloured against white snow and black tree trunks.

It looked warm. And then, strangely, it looked like a flame, more than its own redness showing among the branches, in the twigs, through the needles. A huge red fruit grew in it, hanging round and bright, too hot to look at.

The sun had come through the clouds, rising into the forest, and shone through that one tree directly at Tawena.

"Maneto has spoken," she said. "But I do not know what he has said." She waited. Something else would come, she knew.

It came. There was a whistle, and her bird flew into the tree, looking in the bark for things to eat. The bird with blue wings that had whistled and Rafe had been punished. Tawena laughed at the memory, and the bird whistled again.

Tawena knew where she was now. She knew she was still in her first life, the one she could remember. She knew she had to follow the risen sun, because it rose over the lake. She would find the lake and go on up its western shore and would find new tracks where the Indian women were still taking Rafe to the head of the lake, and round and to his own village. That was what she must do. She had eaten enough food for several days, and she must go at once.

She went without looking back. The past was over. Only the future might be ahead, Maneto promised. She went round the red tree, not wanting to come too close to Maneto's word written on the forest. Beyond that tree she saw the sun struggling among still-snowy boughs, and went towards the point where it had risen.

The forest floor was knee-deep in snow. The surface of the snow lay smooth, though not level. The ground below was rough, hidden, hard. It was a day's walk to the lake shore. Only as darkness came did a straight easy wind blow steadily on her, coming off the lake, not yet slowed or disturbed by the trees.

At the shore ice had formed, and snow lay on the ice. She went across it to free water to drink, and came to land again. There was nothing to eat, but behind a cliff there was a small cave, and everywhere wood for a fire. She sat the night by a fire, warm, and not without hope. She knew what to do, how to find Rafe; all it needed was a long and weary work, an endless and wearing walk. She could find him in spite of new snow and the time that had passed.

The work of finding Rafe was this. She knew that the three in front had walked up the side of the lake, but not close by the shore. Tawena went up the lake after them in big zig-zags, stitching her way along the track she might not see, until at last she did see it. She would then be able to follow it plainly, without having to go from side to side.

Two days and three nights later, days of running the forest, nights of hearing the wolves, she found Rafe. He was sitting by the fireside trying to explain something to the Indian mother, and making strange noises and stranger antics. The woman did not say anything to him, but twisted his face. She was cooking.

Rafe had been making growling noises. Tawena's stomach did the same thing now. She thought that Rafe looked at her, but he was only sitting a little way from the fire and sulking, and a tear fell down his face.

"That was nothing," thought Tawena. "She did not hurt him. Perhaps they are tired of him and will kill him tonight." She hoped that would not happen, because then the women would not take him back to the village. "Perhaps he will kill them. If he does I wonder whether I can take him the rest of the way? White boys are of no use, but I cannot leave him here to die. If these women kill him that is the work of Maneto."

The next night, when Tawena came close to look for scraps to eat, she found Rafe was not there. She knew he was alive. She even felt his bed, and it was warm. He had gone, and he did not come back.

She went to look for him, because it was not right for him to wander alone, by night or by day.

She heard him easily. "It is Rayaf or a bear," she said to herself. "He goes as quietly as he can, like a tree walking."

Rafe was at a stream, hesitating on the edge, his foot a little way into the black water, cold as ice but running too fast to freeze. Then his second foot went in, and he was walking in the water.

"It is clever," said Tawena. "But not wise. The mother and the daughter will still follow him, because he has gone down the current towards the lake, and no one would go anywhere else. However, it is possible they will not trouble to look hard for him. Therefore I shall make him easy to follow, because it is certain he is running away, and that is most foolish, and of no help to me. If I am in the wilderness alone it is nearly too much for me; how much worse it will be for a white boy."

She watched him go out of sight, round a foamy bend in the stream. Then she followed him, but not in the frost-sharp water. She went along the bank, making her track like Rafe's, large and clumsy, breaking twigs and branches, marking the ground, tearing her way through the bushes, pulling snow and moss from the tree trunks and stones by the way.

She made a noise as she went. "It cannot be helped," she thought. "And the worst it will do is drive Rayaf back to

129

the camp. Nevertheless he will not turn because this noise will alarm him."

She followed. She found the track Rafe made when he left the stream, where the lake showed under the sky of very early morning. She looked back on her own track. She had broken through very much the same way.

She followed Rafe as far as he had gone. She climbed a tree and waited. Rafe could not go far, because the lake shore was like teeth sticking up from the water, smooth and steep, and further inland the ground was all chasm and cliff, and the trees grew thick as a blanket. He would stay within earshot.

Later in the day the Indian women came down Tawena's track. They were not looking for Tawena and did not see her. They heard Rafe, and spoke to one another about that. While Rafe struggled half a mile away along the shore the daughter calmly made a fire, the mother methodically caught a fish, and they cooked it.

When night had fallen they went for Rafe. Tawena followed. It was not clear to her that the women would bring him back. She ought to be there to rescue him, if she could, and take him back to his village, and herself as well, if she had to.

The Indian women had left their fire at the darkest part of night. The mother went between Rafe and the water, the daughter beyond him. The daughter then came close to him and made something like the noise of a wolf, so that he ran away down the steep undergrowth, and when he did so the mother caught him.

Then Tawena saw that they would never kill him, except to save him from something worse. She saw how the mother held him as if he were her own child, taking his face and looking into his eyes; and how the daughter led him to where the fire was, and the fish ready to eat, while he sobbed and bubbled between them.

Then, for a time, Tawena thought she might come out from hiding and speak to the women, and join in a family once more, and have something more than the company of wolves, the stern silence of Maneto, or the whistle of the bird with blue wings, when it came.

"All the same, I know they should take a knife to me," she said. "I am alive now, even if I am not fully happy. Maybe, and I do not know, if I were dead I should not even feel that."

Instead she hurried back to the women's camp and ate all the food she could find there, untidily, like some animal, going off into the woods afterwards to sleep.

Two days later, very uneasy at a new smell in the forest, she went ahead of the people she was following. She knew the smell that came from the land ahead. It was horses and men, white men and their own horses, their guns, their leather, their food, their fire.

The Indian women were uneasy too. They stayed the day among some rocks, listening. After the sun had begun silently to sink and the middle of the day had come and gone, the daughter went forward to look, to see what was ahead.

"It is no good thing," thought Tawena. "They will give that boy to white men, and never go to the village. And I, I dare not go near the white people alone. Maneto, why have you brought me close to enemies all round me?"

She followed the daughter, not wanting to go close to white people alone. She wondered whether the daughter knew she was there, and decided that she only looked about her so, and listened often, because she was hunting, and because of the white men. So they stayed separate, coming to the white man's camp at the same time, a little way apart. The woman had killed a small deer as she came, and laid it in a joint of tree branches out of the way, while she came to the white man's camp.

131

"It does not matter if she sees me now," said Tawena to herself. "She will think I am following the white man, perhaps a slave."

The white men's camp was dirty, smelly, and noisy. There were fires far larger than anyone could need, there were good bones being dropped into the flames half-eaten. The ground was trampled and torn, and no one looked out at the forest.

"It is very likely that no one would come near," thought Tawena. "All the same, we have."

She saw food being cooked, and was hungry. It seemed to her that it would be easy to get some of that food, because no one watched, no one looked. And it did not matter if the daughter of the Indian mother saw her here, at this place.

A better watch was being kept than she knew. She had no sooner started to cross the open space at the edge of the clearing where the camp stood, than a rifle was raised and a shot fired.

Tawena thought she was dead there and then. But the bullet did not reach her. It passed over her head. It had not been meant to kill, only to frighten.

The bullet went by and hit a tree a glancing blow, shaking the stem so that a shower of raindrops fell from it. The tree continued to shake and the branches to sway like the wings of a bird.

The bullet went singing off into the forest.

"Maneto has done it for me," thought Tawena, safe again among the trees, lying flat on the pine needles. "Maneto shakes a tree for me again."

The Indian woman had gone too. Tawena looked round for her. She found what she had not expected, a pool of blood, and leading from it the sick, uncareful walk of the woman as she made her way back towards her mother and Rafe at the camp.

"I have done this," said Tawena. "In spite of all, if one of them dies the other will not take the white boy to his own village. May Maneto snap the white man's gun like a rotten bow."

And she followed, slowly, the slow walking of the Indian woman as she went hurt to her own fireside.

"If she should fall," she said to herself, "I shall bring the other woman to her, and they will kill me. Perhaps that bullet is for both of us, but Maneto does not want the white man to know he has succeeded."

nineteen

The Indian woman did not fall. She stopped walking and stood against a tree. If the tree had not been there she would have fallen. She dropped the deer, and it fell like an empty bag. Tawena waited for her to move, to walk again, to fall, but she did not.

"She has died," said Tawena to herself. "If that is so then that is so. Tapwa, it is true."

But sleep is like death. Tawena went on watching. She was not certain what to do.

"It may be a trap," she thought. "Perhaps she is now lying in wait for me, and if I go to her she will take me, and since I have no cheek-cuts she will no longer let me live. Or perhaps she is dying herself, and in that case the other woman, her mother, will surely, tapwa, leave Rayaf dead among the trees, or will leave him and know that he will die. At the end of it all, can I bring Rayaf to his own village? I cannot make my way there alone. Will it be worse with Rayaf, or better? I cannot tell."

There was nothing that could be right, no way of saving herself. "Ah, Maneto," she said, out loud, "I have done nothing in my life, good or bad, that can be remembered. Why then do you let me live so long, only to take me away? But if you are coming, then come soon."

And she sat herself against a tree and waited for Maneto to come for her, or send one of his creatures.

"Perhaps," she thought, "I have taken the name of Bear when I should not, and Bear will come. I shall wait." She laid the knife on the ground in front of her, to show that she would not use it on Bear, or any creature Maneto sent.

Maneto seemed to send a very small creature. Down from among the trees dropped the bird with blue wings, looking at the ground. The bird whistled, looking at Tawena with one eye, at the forest with the other. It whistled again, and flew off towards the Indian woman, who stood like a tree against a tree.

Near her it whistled again. When it did so the Indian woman turned her head and looked. She saw the bird. The bird saw her with one eye, Tawena with the other. The woman seemed to see right through the bird's head, seeing what it saw with the other eye.

She saw Tawena. Tawena saw her eyes, not through the bird, but across the glade.

So Maneto had spoken, through the bird with blue wings. Tawena had been seen, sitting in full view, waiting to die. The Indian woman spoke, but no words came.

Tawena picked up the knife and went to her. She would not leave the knife while she was alive. "But we do not know Maneto," she said. "He knows us."

"My mother," said the Indian woman, slowly, her hand like bone on a branch of the tree, holding her up.

"She thinks I am her mother," thought Tawena.

It was not so, she found a moment later. The Indian woman knew she was another person. "My mother," she said again, "waits for me." She brought her hand from the tree and held Tawena's shoulder. "But we must not call. Maneto will hear, and I am not ready to go with Maneto. The white man has thrown a bullet at me, that is all."

Tawena pulled herself alongside the woman, took her good arm on her shoulder, and helped her walk, dragging the deer, because it should have gone over the shoulders the woman leaned on.

"The pain," said the woman, "is not the worst pain. But my soul has run out of the wound and taken away my strength."

Tawena knew that food was for strength, but there was no food here, apart from the deer, and it was not the time to cook that. The bird with blue wings flew round them both, and it found food now and then in the bark of trees or on the ground.

The road back was two miles long, but it took the time of ten. The daylight was falling from the sky when Tawena smelt old smoke among the trees, among the rocks that made this place different from the rest of the forest.

The woman rested for a time now, her back against a rock. Tawena left her and scouted along down the smell of old smoke. She saw the other woman and Rafe, waiting, waiting, Rafe not very still, the Indian mother still and listening. They had firewood in a great white man's sort of stack, but no fire. The tent was still folded. Tawena went round behind a rock and climbed it, to look down on the camp from higher up.

When she reached the top, and worked herself to the edge, she saw the wounded woman walk into the camp. The tent was put up, Rafe lit the fire, a smoky one because he did not know how to make a clean blaze. He then cut up the deer, but quite spoilt the skin by ripping it with the stone knife.

"I wish," said Tawena, "that I had taken something from that deer when I carried it and had the knife ready." She had to live on the smell of it while others cooked and ate it.

In the morning Rafe was sent for firewood. Tawena could not believe he was so stupid in the way he behaved. He lost his way because he could not follow his own tracks. He could not turn round and go back the way he had come. He could not tell when he crossed the path he had made. He hauled his firewood about the forest, and did not know where he was.

Tawena drove him back to the camp. She wanted to be able to come out and say she was there. She wanted to be sure she could go to the women and not be killed. She thought that perhaps she could, that perhaps they would forgive her, somehow, for not having cheek-cuts, but she could not be sure. The younger one, she was sure, had said nothing, perhaps had forgotten her, perhaps thought she was a dream of weakness. But if she appeared quite real, in front of them both, they might do as they should, and take her life away. There was no need to ask Maneto. Tawena stayed hidden, making bear noises to send Rafe to the camp again.

At the camp they did not believe there had been a bear; but no one came hunting Tawena.

During the day the bullet was taken from the daughter. She shrieked like the rubbing of one branch against another in a great storm, shrieked once and that was all. The rest of the day was spent waiting for the daughter to be well again.

In the morning the camp was taken up, and the fire put out. When Tawena had seen all three of them well gone she went to the site and searched for remains of food. She found a bundle of twigs and leaves, and smelt inside it meat. It was some of the solid back of the deer.

First she felt a great fear, that the mother would come back for what they had left and discover her taking what had been forgotten. Then she felt a greater one, that this bundle of food was the bait in a trap, and she was already tricked and caught.

Then she had a third thought, and that seemed the best one, not of fear but the greatest comfort, and she wanted to believe it.

"The daughter has remembered me," she told herself. "No doubt that is the case. There is no need for my back to feel cold with fear. She has remembered me, and although I have no cheek-cuts she has not sent death to me, but instead has given me a gift, knowing I am near. That is good, but no doubt it is the last of her thanks, and I shall stay out of sight."

She took the bundle of meat and went into the forest with it, to eat it where she could not be found. Then she slept, as animals do after eating.

She found the trail easily, and followed it up. When the sun was highest she almost ran into the next camp, where the travellers had stopped a whole day, in a place where Tawena herself would not have stayed, too close to water, too near a flood if one came, too easy to see if someone looked. Tawena had not been looking or she would not have come close enough to see the daughter lying in the open tent, poisoned with a fever and in great pain.

"She will die, after all," Tawena thought. "Is there no good end to all that happens, Maneto?"

Maneto did not answer. Tawena watched. To her surprise Rafe came to look after the daughter, cooking something at the fire first.

"She will not eat," thought Tawena. "She is too sick, and no person will eat that moss from the marshes. This is foolishness."

However, the moss was not for eating. Rafe boiled it,

then wrung it dry, and laid it on the daughter's shoulder, and left her once more. The mother sat by the fire.

Not long afterwards the daughter spoke, and the mother came to her. It was plain that the fever had left the daughter, that the poison had left the wound. At night she drank tea and ate fish.

When Rafe went to his bed, after putting yet more moss on the shoulder, the mother came to him and spoke with her hands on his face. She spoke kind words of thanks with her lips, too. Rafe did not know the words themselves but he knew what was meant. Tawena saw how tears of joy and happiness rose in his eyes.

"White boys have a soul that shows, perhaps," said Tawena. "I do not have much soul, and that is why Maneto does not send for me."

Yet if she had no soul at all, why were there some tears of longing in her eyes too? She did not ask the question very clearly, because she did not know how much she longed to be like Rafe, living among her own people.

She went away into the forest alone, very much alone. "I am alive," she said to the bird with blue wings, "but not as I want to be. I cannot say who I am, and no one I see cares for me. Sometimes I think it would be better if I went to the Indian women, because to be kept by them would be better than bad; to be slain by them would be bad only; but to be alone and see them, lonely and watching, is the worst thing."

She sat and looked at the far distance, down a valley among the trees, where nothing moved. Inside her head, and in her chest, something struggled. She knew that if she did not hold it back she would weep, and she would not do that.

Her eyes grew wet, in spite of all she did, and everything she looked at swelled and shifted, and she had to sniff.

When she did so she smelt a new smell among the trees,

something she did not know. A creature new to her was nearby. She breathed with nose and mouth, tasting the air. The sadness that had been inside her, trying to get out, was pushed aside, forgotten. In her chest her heart began to beat, she began to be ready for danger. An unknown thing is likely to be danger.

Her eyes stopped changing the shape of the forest, stopped making trees move. But something moved, coming up the little valley, upright, looking from side to side, carrying a stick like a club, like half a tree.

Tawena froze completely still when she saw it and half-closed her eyes, so that light would not shine from them. The thing coming was taller than a man, not twice as tall but halfway to that, like one man on another's shoulders. It was only one creature, however. It walked, striding the long paces of a giant. It wore no clothes, though it was manlike. It was covered in fur, bearded round the face, and had fingers like a man.

"Bigfoot," said Tawena, deep in her mind, silently. Now she was no longer afraid, but still careful. Bigfoot was so shy, lived so much alone in secret places, that no one knew all his behaviour. He did not kill to eat; that was all Tawena knew. He was harmless and meant to be left alone, but care had to be taken, because any creature will act wildly if it is startled.

Bigfoot trod his way closer, thinking he was alone. Then his eyes met Tawena's, perhaps because she had opened hers. He saw her. At once he turned away, going up the far side of the valley, walking fast, ten-foot swings to each leg; and then he ran. For a long time Tawena watched him; for a long way she saw his great prints on the snow.

"He is more alone than I," said Tawena to herself. "It is clear that Maneto has spoken to me again. I am to be content as I am; that is the rule."

She went back towards the camp, ready to follow at a

distance, to watch from afar; to walk the other way, like Bigfoot, if she was likely to be seen.

All the same, during the night, not being quite sure, she crept to Rafe's side and curled up there for a time, wanting to speak, wanting to let him know she was there, wanting to be asked to come and stay. Rafe, being a white boy, knew she was some wild animal, and became stiff with fright.

Not far away the wolves ran again about the forest, and Bigfoot roamed silent and solitary.

twenty

Some days later, going slowly at first while the Indian
daughter recovered her strength, they all reached a river
that could not be crossed at that point. It was too wide, too
rapid, too fierce. Tawena reckoned it was the big river
running in at the head of the lake, and that beyond it they
would turn back towards the village, which was on that
side. They would be going down the other side of the lake.
First they had to travel to a crossing place.

The way upriver was in open land, where the Indian
women cut across a big river bend, through grass country.
Tawena had to keep further away on this part of the
journey, where there was little cover for a follower. To be
safe she struck a path further from the river, and followed
from one side, not from behind.

She was lucky with the weather, a thick mist covering
her, and the others, and every animal.

One night, having come during the day such a great
distance, and being hungry still, she curled under the only

bush she had seen, and went to sleep.

She was woken in the dark by a puffing, grunting noise, and by a gentle shaking of the ground. A large animal was moving nearby. Or several large animals were moving a little distance off. She lay still and waited, while the misty landscape round her grew brighter.

Before she could see what was there she smelt it. There were buffalo here, the herd moving up during the night or just before dawn. She saw the big rumps of the cows, the great shaggy shoulders of the bulls, the horns wider than a man could reach.

Then, gently, a huge head and wide nose discovered her under the bush that the large mouth was about to eat, and breathed on her. The buffalo sniffed at her several times, sang a shaking song in its throat, and put its nose under her, turning her over, somersaulting her out on to the grass, getting her out of the way. The animal's whole head then ate the bush.

Other members of the herd came to see what Tawena was, sniffing at her one by one, dribbling on her, turning her over once or twice more, eating a length of the hem from the brown village dress, sucking the hair from her head. Tawena was kicked, coughed at, not quite trodden on, almost sat on, and ignored. The herd settled round her, some lying down to chew their cud, others grazing. The sun came up and the mist went away. Tawena crawled towards the sun, eastward, towards the river. She crawled the best part of a mile before she was out of the buffalo herd, now and then having to stop for weariness, now and then because some animal thought she should be investigated and dealt with, tasted and teased.

Before she was free of them all she heard the river, pushing its way through some narrow place, thundering, making the ground quiver. Ahead was a big smoke. She thought at first there might be a town there, then knew it was the spray from a great waterfall.

The two women and Rafe were nowhere in sight. Tawena carefully came to their track. It was a fresh track, leaves uncurling from being trodden on, Rafe's clumsy mark on a stone still wet.

The trail led down to the river, to the greatest noise, to the waterfall itself. Here the ground shivered all the time, the noise raved in the air, and nothing else could be heard.

"They have thrown him in," thought Tawena. "They will therefore throw me in too. But if they have thrown him in where are they themselves?"

She looked more closely. The trail faded beside the waterfall, because the splash washed down and cleared the signs away. Tawena trod in the slimy mud and went down on her back for fifteen or twenty feet, towards the falling water, to the cliff top where it fell many times the height of a man, many times the height of Bigfoot, down to the lower valley.

A ledge of rock saved her. She hung on to a root. Cold water slapped and dripped. Under her feet was the depth. Against her back was rock. In front of her was water, and the water was falling, falling, falling, and since it was so much bigger than everything else it seemed to Tawena that she and the ground she could feel (quite a lot of it hurting her back) were rising up, going up, floating up, and the water was keeping still.

Behind the water, when she had made the ground understand that it stood still, and that the water moved, she saw a sort of cave, one side rock, the other water. On the back wall of it she saw the scrape of a hand, where someone had held on.

She slid and slipped her way to the cave, finding it like a tunnel, mud underfoot, a muddied wall on the left, and a great curtain of water, like some enormous tent-flap, on the other side.

"Maneto's tent has a flap like that," she said. If she spoke aloud she did not hear what she said. The noise of the fall did not only make more noise than could be heard; it got inside her head from other places than her ears, and shook her teeth and eyes. She felt it got into her heart and stopped her thinking.

She thought enough to know that the others had come this way. No doubt this was the place to cross the river, but if it was not she would meet them as they came back.

"If that is so," she felt, or thought, or said, "I shall give the knife to Rayaf and be sent into the water."

The tunnel curved, going back into the cliff towards the middle of the river. As she came round the curve she saw, with a sudden extra chill to her body, that the three of them were ahead. The light coming through the water was dimmed, the air in the tunnel was full of spray, so she could not tell at first which way the party was moving. She found that there would be enough time for her to escape if necessary, and then she saw clearly that the others were going away from her, right through the passage to the other side.

The mother, who led the way, stood in brighter light beyond the tunnel; Rafe followed her, and last came the daughter.

When Tawena reached the end herself, coming out into sunlight, they had moved on. They had not gone far, but were standing on a cliff path, looking ahead and looking back, and that was all.

By now Tawena was used to the shuddering noise of the fall. She could hear sounds beyond it. There was nothing much to hear, the tumbling of occasional rock, the cracking of a falling stone in the water itself, the movements of her own feet. These were things of no help or meaning.

She had to take another path. She did not want to stand in the showering water of the fall any longer. She took a way lower down the cliff, going from hanging root to clinging grass, to tussock of reed and knot of creeper, below, out of sight of the rest.

She saw what was holding the others still, why they were not moving. On their path stood a bear. He was not wanting to go along the path (nothing would have stopped him if he had wanted to), but he did not intend to get off it either. He was sending snarls and growls to the women and Rafe. He saw Tawena and showed teeth to her too, standing up on his ledge and scraping the cliff with huge claws.

Tawena went back and lower still, almost down to the river, where she would be out of sight of the women and the bear. Behind her the river fell off a cliff top, plunged down, and boiled at the bottom of the cliff. That was all over, and she let the sound of it go from her head.

She stood and thought, breathing deep, remembering, working out what to do, what first, what next. She was now going to do what she had intended when she went with Rafe to look at the bear's winter den on the headland.

Then she had meant to stand outside while the bear was only half awake and tease him by making sounds like another bear, a she-bear, to make him call back. Then, before he came, she and Rayaf were going to run home, laughing at what they had done, leaving the bear to go to sleep again.

That had gone wrong because the bear had been disturbed by the ice mounting up on the headland, shifting his den. He had come out too soon, too angry, too hungry.

Now Tawena was about to do the same thing, but with the bear already fully awake, probably already looking for a she-bear, and with Tawena herself having nowhere to go if anything went wrong.

She began the calls, the whimpers and yelps of a she-bear. She started by feeling extremely like a bear herself, and went on almost to the point of climbing up the broken cliff and going to the bear.

She stopped, very suddenly, because behind her, down by the water, there was a very unpleasant noise indeed. She knew when she heard it that the bear on the cliff was indeed already looking for a she-bear, and had already heard her. Now Tawena heard her too, coming up from the water's edge, giving bear shouts to warn Tawena off, because one bear and one she-bear were enough.

At the same time the bear himself was coming down from the cliff. Tawena stopped being a bear in every way, and became an Indian girl who had been teasing bears, and the bears were coming. She ran, scrambling over boulders, pushing among branches, not caring how she was hurt by doing so, knowing that what a bear did would be very much worse.

They followed her, but not for long. Very soon they began to argue with one another, and Tawena felt safe.

In a calm pond at the edge of the river she found fresh-water mussels, and cracked them open with the knife, making a meal by daylight. The sunlight went and clouds came, and she curled up away from the water behind a tree stump, hoping next morning to dig out wood-worms for a meal then. After that she would find the trail of the Indian women and Rafe.

In the night she woke, thinking that the bears had caught up with her. But it was not that. The wind blew up from the lake, then stopped. When it did so she heard some far-off thing moving, approaching, some huge thing, larger by far than Bigfoot, huger even than the waterfall, and more frightening.

"Maneto knows," she said. But she was not sure of that. Maneto might know, but he could not deal with all the things in the world: that was too much.

In the suddenly still air the thing was big. Tawena heard

it tramp through the trees, because the forest ran the same on this side of the river as it had on the other. She heard the trees snap and fall, she heard them thrown aside.

There was only one thing that could do that, one thing that walked the forest breaking it down, one thing that no one had seen and lived to talk about. That thing was the Wendagoo. No one lived to speak of it, because if it came on a man, woman, child, horse, ox, buffalo, dog, it would eat them. Most of all it liked men, women, and children. No one that saw it had ever come back.

She was sure she had sinned once too often, offended Bear by teasing him, at last, to his own face in his own land. Maneto had stood aside and let Wendagoo happen.

In the still silence the Wendagoo came on. The ground began to thump, hard enough to move Tawena, lifting her and dropping her an inch or two. Nearer and nearer came the breaking of the trees, the crushing of trunks and branches, their falling to the ground.

Tawena shut her eyes. But the Wendagoo would smell her, she knew, would sniff her out, and put her in its mouth, and no one would ever know. She opened her eyes, thinking she would see what it was that ate her.

The Wendagoo came up the hillside. Tawena saw the trees falling, because the night was not quite dark. She saw the tops lean to one side and go over. She saw them lifted and fall away from the place where they had grown. In the calm air the sound of the Wendagoo was like a great howling of a thousand wolves. She saw it, the Wendagoo itself, rising high into the sky, tall, black, swaying, walking among the trees as if they were grass, coming towards her.

The air stopped being still. She began to be pulled towards the Wendagoo, its great voice seemed to draw her in, to be sucking her up to itself. It stood, black, with strange flashing and sparklings inside it, not far from her.

148

It retreated. It left her. It had other things to do, other places to walk.

It went by, not coming close enough to take her. It did not eat her; she was still alive. She had seen the Wendagoo and had lived.

But it did not mean that she would ever tell anyone, because there was still no one to tell. Perhaps there would not be. She did not know. Maneto had not told her.

Maneto spoke, in his own way. There was a flutter close by, and a whistle. The bird with blue wings had come again, bringing her its message.

The Wendagoo climbed the hill, then left the ground, taking wing and going up into the clouds. On the ground was the place it had walked in, broken and torn. Beside it Tawena slept again, and the woken bird waited for dawn.

twenty-one

Peaceful days followed for Tawena. She knew the village was only a long walk away. The snow went completely and the days grew longer. On nearly every one of them she found food, small animals running carelessly in grassy clearings, new leaves showing where old fat roots could be dug up with the knife, eggs by the waterside, flowers that could be sucked for a taste of honey.

The Indian women moved on slowly. Tawena thought they were still undecided what to do, whether to leave Rayaf on his own and go to their own people, without going to the strange village. Tawena did not fret about that now. She knew she could get Rafe home alone if she had to. She knew she must if she could.

She smelt the village, on a south wind, two days before Rafe did, the strong rooms and iron of all the white people.

She saw Rafe become dressed like an Indian boy. She saw him using a small bow and hitting what he aimed at, some of the time.

One day Rafe saw a man and a dog a long way off, and was pleased to have done so well. Tawena was much nearer the dog, and the dog came to look at her. She and the knife knew what to do. The man walked on alone. Tawena carried the dog three miles, cooked it, and ate it. The eating took her two days. On the third she ran for a long time and caught up with Rafe and the women.

She was sure now that Rafe could get home alone. He had only to stand still and he would be found. He had only to walk and he would be heard by an Indian. She went past him and the women, and came to her own tent at the far side of the village.

"You have been dead many days," said her mother.

"I have been killed many times," said Tawena. "I have seen the Wendagoo. Yet Maneto spoke, and I have come back."

"We have been beaten many times because a white boy is lost," said her mother, looking at her for the truth.

"Rayaf will be here tomorrow," said Tawena. "With some women to whom I could not speak, having no cuts on my cheeks. I have his knife," she remembered, talking of cuts.

"Give it back or we shall be beaten again," said her mother.

"I wish to do so," said Tawena.

Her journey was over. She was still reasonably full of white man's fat dog, and went to sleep for a long time. Her brothers and sisters, all younger, remembered and forgot her, and walked about in her dreams.

The next day she saw Rafe come into the village. She knew he was a white boy, walking still like Bear. The men at the gate thought he was Indian, and their guns, without rising up, seemed to point to him.

The women were alarmed at being in the village at all, alarmed and ashamed. Tawena looked at them hard, without hiding. She knew they must come. She had told them to do so, and they had. They had come because there would be a reward. It looked as if they knew exactly what they wanted. Now that Rafe was back here they did not expect, and would not understand, any fuss to be made of them. They would expect to be given a fair reward.

Rafe went into his own house, where the same crow hopped on the roof. He came out half an hour later with his mother. Tawena felt it was safe now for her to be seen by the women. She stood round the corner of the house, and watched. The daughter looked at her, touched her own cheeks, and said nothing. Tawena touched her own left shoulder. That, for them, was a long conversation, with much meaning.

After that many people were about, and more talk than there could be meaning for. The Indian women got what they asked for, a horse, and a travoy, a bag of flour and one of tobacco. Rafe's father shook his head at the expense. Then everyone held the hands of all the others, but there was no fighting, which was what Tawena expected next. The mother rode the horse, the daughter sat on the poles.

Rafe went indoors then. Tawena dared not go to the house with the knife. Mrs Considine would have shut the door against her, sure she meant mischief. White people's doors were always locked. They did not understand friendly interest. Tawena waited not far from the house.

Later in the afternoon, while all the other boys were still in school, she saw Rafe come out of the house.

Rafe only saw one of the tent Indians come by, a small thin girl, ragged and dirty.

"Rayaf," she said, which did not surprise him, because everyone knew his name and that was how the Indians said it. And she gave him a knife without a sheath.

Rafe knew the knife. It was his own. On the leather rings of the handle was his own sign, R for Rafe. It was the very knife Tawena had stolen from him, the one his father had made.

How it came here he could not understand. How this Indian girl could have it he had no idea. He did not know her. They knew him, but he did not always know them, down in the tents at the end of the village.

This thin girl looked at him. "It's my knife," he said, and took it from her. "Thank you," he said, clearly not knowing whether she would understand.

She seemed not to. She walked on. Rafe looked at the spoilt blade of the knife, chipped, blunted, rusted. It was almost not worth having back. There were dog hairs on the guard of the blade. The knife had been used for digging. And for what else? But how could it have come back here, to his hand, when he had lost it the far side of the lake, so many weeks since?

The girl went some way off. She stopped and looked at him again.

"Rayaf," she said once more. Then she began an extraordinary thing. She leaned forward and pointed her elbows out, and took a deep breath. She bent her legs a little. She made a noise like a bear snuffing and hunting. Somehow she made the noise of its claws on wood. She took another breath and screamed.

Rafe had heard a scream like that in the woods, when Tawena had been killed by the bear. He wished this girl did not know the story and remind him.

After the scream the girl made more bear noises; and she went on to make the noises that Tawena had made out in the darkness, as well as those of the bear, including the snapping crunch of the last bite that killed her.

Rafe listened and hated it all. He disliked being reminded of how he had done nothing; detested remembering how frightened he had been; he hated to think how he had not cared at the time, that he had not wanted to do anything for Tawena, had not cared if she died.

But how could this girl know about it? There was a thought beginning to come into Rafe's mind, though it could not be so.

The girl in the street in the village now began a sort of howling speech. That again was something Rafe had heard. It was the speech of the bear to Deerskin and Hareskin, when it had told them to take him, not to slavery, but to his own village.

And here he was, returned to his own village. There was only one Indian girl who could know about what had happened, only one person in the world.

"Tawena," he said. "Tawena."

"Rayaf," said the girl. "Tawena."

It was Tawena. She no longer had the fat cheeks of the tent girl, which were the things he had known her best by. Nevertheless, she was Tawena.

"But," said Rafe, "you were killed."

She came closer to him and showed her arm. She took the knife again and laid it the length of a long scar, and that was how she had bled the stain on the snow. All the fight with the bear had been unreal, all to lead to the words the bear spoke, all to make Deerskin and Hareskin bring Rafe back home unharmed.

"Tawena follow Rayaf, Indian womans," said Tawena. "All ever day. Tawena light fire for Rayaf. Tawena walk like bear for Rayaf, watch him. Tawena sleep by Rayaf some ever nights. Tawena follow through big water and call bear away. Tawena follow ever time. Easy follow Rayaf," and she walked a few clumsy steps, like Rafe not following in Deerskin's footprints.

"Thank you," said Rafe. "It was very kind of you. You are a good girl."

"No ever good Tawena," said Tawena. "Indian womans take Rayaf home, I follow, me home too. Me ever home, so

154

Rayaf thank you. Indian womans kill Tawena."

Then she went, leaving Rafe startled and wondering. She had saved herself by saving him. And he had not saved her at all.

"Will you come in, Rafe," said Mrs Considine. "Don't be talking to them Indian girls."

"That's the one that I went with," said Rafe. "But she helped me all she could."

"That sort doesn't," said Mrs Considine. "Come to your supper, you're as lean as a bed, and wandering in your wits. Aren't they all alike, Indian children?"

Rafe went in. But always he remembered the noise of the bear in the woods, the fire mysteriously lit, the foot-prints of bear; and mostly the presence once or twice by night of Tawena beside him.

Tawena went away with other Indians during the summer. Rafe was never sure whether she came back. She never spoke to him again, if she did.

"Women," said his father, when he spoke of it; and Mrs Considine said, when Rafe angered her again, "Wouldn't I rather have the bag of meal and them Indians have kept you!"